The Storm & the Sea

Also by R. D. G. Lover

Angels' Compass
Tempest of Angels
Inheriting Armageddon

The Tides of Amelia Island
The Storm & the Sea
Rose Tide & Rust

the wisteria collection
wisteria, vol. I

Coloring Books
The Amelia Island Coloring Book

A Tides of Amelia Island Novel

R. D. G. LOVER

4pocalypse Arts

4pocalypse Arts

This book is a work of fiction. Any references to historical events, real people, or real places are used fictitiously. Other names, characters, places, and events are product of the author's imagination, and any resemblance to actual events or places or persons, living or dead, is entirely coincidental.

First Paperback Edition December 2024

For information about special discounts for bulk purchases or to book an event with the author, please contact R. D. G. Lover at www.4pocalypsearts.com or via email at racheldglover@gmail.com.

ISBN 979-8-9904778-1-0

*To all the girls who feel like a hurricane—
you are devastatingly beautiful. Embrace it.*

He stilled the storm to a whisper;
the waves of the sea were hushed.

Psalm 107:29 NIV

Playlist

I Miss You (feat. Julia Michaels) | Clean Bandit
Whiskey | Young Rising Sons
Ocean | Parachute
Didn't I | OneRepublic
The Heat | The Score
One Too Many | Keith Urban, P!nk
Don't Tell Me | Phillip Phillips
Hotter Than Hell | Dua Lipa
Teeth In Me | Jonathan Tilkin
Burnt Sugar | Felicity
Devil's Backbone | The Civil Wars
I'm The Sinner | Jared Benjamin
Chicago | Win and Woo, Bryce Fox
Breaking Inside (feat. Lzzy Hale) | Shinedown
Dirty Mind | Boy Epic
W A R | John Michael Howell
Killer | Valerie Broussard
Poison | SICK PUPPIES
Not Strong Enough | Apocalyptica, Brent Smith
Wanted Is Love | Phillip Phillips
Rescue Me | Daughtry
Gravity | Matt Hansen
Deja Vu | James Arthur
Another Place | Bastille, Alessia Cara

Always Remember Us This Way | Noelle Johnson
Dearly Beloved | Daughtry
Roots | Valerie Broussard, Galantis
Beautiful Things | Benson Boone
Stargazing | Myles Smith
I'll Follow You | Shinedown

Author's Note

I WOULD LIKE TO START by saying that this story is honestly just fanfiction of my own characters from my fantasy book series, Angels' Compass, which is about the Four Horsemen of the Apocalypse as karaoke-loving, motorcycle-riding, hipster assassins. I pursued traditional publishing for the first book in Angels' Compass, called *Inheriting Armageddon,* for years, racking up over one hundred rejections. Nevertheless, this story is my passion project and where my heart truly lies.

The characters from Angels' Compass don't get *happily ever afters* in their stories. This specific trilogy of novels (The Tides of Amelia Island) was inspired by the creativity and drama of Amelia Island, which lead me to give my characters HEAs in an alternate universe. Why not?

I have not changed the name of the island or major establishments in the area. Amelia Island has always been magical to me, and even though I respect the concept of changing names and locations for the sake of fiction, I wanted to keep everything the same in this novel to fully immerse myself (and you as a reader) in the story.

Lastly, there are somewhat spicy scenes in this novel. There is alcohol use. There are brief scenes of child abuse. One of the characters is a foster child who experiences abandonment issues into her adult life. If these things are triggering or sensitive topics for you, please consider recommending this novel to a friend who might like it instead.

I would also like to say that I do not endorse any of the actions of my characters. Please don't drink and drive. Please be *responsible* when you drink. Lastly, please don't risk your life having hurricane parties in Florida.

Chapter One

KATRINA

You know what it feels like, running from a storm, only to get caught in the downpour? That's what it feels like, running from him.

I open the car door, and humid air rushes in. My legs still thrum with the rhythm of the interstate from the sixteen-hour drive. It feels good to be done with the night. My adrenaline has finally caved after the nonstop trip from Illinois to Florida, but hell, do I finally feel *free.*

I step out into the clammy Florida air and breathe deep. It smells of salt and pine and rain.

The parking lot around me is half full. It isn't quite summer yet, so not everyone has flocked to the destination state. Darkness blots the colors of the cars and the hotel into one muddied navy blue. But one thing is full of light.

I look up.

Above me, the sky shines with millions of stars. With no streetlights and only a measly, dim, orange hotel light in my periphery, I can see each and every one of them.

Breath rushes from my lungs.

You've never seen so many stars in your life.

My city life was a flood of stars in its own right. Man-made stars.

This is a different sort of feeling. Peace. There is no rush, no chaos, no corporate ladder to climb, no *pressure.*

I smile.

Chapter Two

KATRINA

THREE MONTHS LATER

THE BUSTLE OF THE RESTAURANT clamors in my ears. The kitchen behind me hollers out order numbers. I alternate between grabbing empty drink cups and slinging a damp towel from my shoulder onto the glossy tables. I sweep away crumbs as quickly as I can with one hand, balance a tray in the other.

The towel flicks back to my shoulder. I slip four menus out of my apron and slide them across the newly cleaned table.

"Katrina!" Jackson calls from across the bar.

I look up, meeting my boss's eyes.

Jackson beams back with a grin like wildfire. His dyed-red hair contrasts with his dark skin, his expression uniquely jovial. No one has a smile like Jackson. He smiles like each day is his biggest feat yet, something I envy deeply. I wish I could smile like that, but it's something I've yet to learn.

In time you will, I think to myself as I walk over.

"Do you mind closing up tonight?" Jackson asks.

"Not at all," I respond without a second thought. "I need the money, anyway." I tuck a stray strand of hair behind my ear, which has fallen in my rush around the floor.

"Be careful, alright?" Jackson says. "I can come back and lock up if you need me to, but my sister needs me to pick her kid up from soccer practice."

"I'll be alright. Thanks, boss," I say with a smile. Call me stupid, but I feel *safe* after dark, closing up the restaurant on my own. Something about this place, this island, feels so much safer than Chicago—almost stupidly safe. It's good. A change. My smile falters. Thoughts creep back in: all the ways I lived on the edge there—work, finances, *love.* So many mistakes. A clean break was always for the better, and I don't regret that choice now. *Safety is* for the better.

Jackson thanks me then returns to the bar where he continues tending to his customers.

I nod to myself. *Yes. Safety is for the better. This is for the best.*

But another voice whispers to me, too. *Don't you miss the danger? Don't you miss me?*

His voice.

I shake my head.

Then I shake my head again to try to rid myself of the feeling completely. People will think I'm crazy if I keep nodding and shaking randomly. I hurry back into the kitchen with my dirty tray, ditch it in the sink, then slip past the other employees and step out back into the parking lot. Fresh air is good for many things—something I'm learning more and more each day.

I drink in the feeling of the sun on my skin, and it warms me to my core. It's nothing like the cold I used to know, the type that bites and gnaws at your bones. This is new. I'm almost convinced the sun can heal anything.

When I first started my job at the waterfront diner, I hadn't thought much of it, but as time went on, I realized the job filled a hole in my heart I hadn't really known was there. I love my coworkers, and I love my boss. They look after me—a welcome change from my previous barista job up north. There, everything had been a free-for-all, every man for himself. Here, I guess, there is some sort of truth to "Southern charm."

I stick my head back into the kitchen and catch a whiff of hot oil and deep-fried breading. I tell the kitchen I'm going to take five and slip away after I get a nod of acknowledgment.

This is what I love most about my job: the casual way everyone works. Everyone does their job, but a five-minute break isn't cause for discipline.

I round the building on cobblestone steps to the marina that flanks the diner. As I clear the sky-blue stucco building, the wind catches my hair and lifts it off my shoulders. The warm breeze is like fingers trailing over my skin, leaving tacky kisses in their wake.

For a second, I debate pulling my ponytail out and letting my wild, curly hair free. As a waiter, I don't have to net my hair, but Jackson requests I keep it pulled back. *It's fine. Every job has its setbacks. This is minimal.*

I listen to the *thump* of my heels against the wood dock as I walk to the railing. I gaze over the view—the crystal-still water, the ever-crossing lines of sailboat masts and sail lines. I wonder to myself if someone were to make a mosaic of the view, if the artist would choose all different colors to fill those small spots of the sky. It's another welcome thought. This town is full of artists, a skill I had never given a second thought. Now, being surrounded by such creativity, I find myself looking through a similar lens.

My break will be over soon, still something about this place captivates me. There is something familiar about the river, about the coast, about being this close to the ocean—a feeling like standing on the edge of the world.

THE REST OF MY SHIFT blows by. One at a time, my coworkers clock out until I'm the only one left.

The diner is uncharacteristically quiet. Bar stools are tucked under the U-shaped bar that sits in the middle of the floor. Booths are cleaned. Sinks are empty. The cash register at the bar gapes open, no cash in sight. Beyond the wrap-around bay windows, the evening peeks in, moonlight reflecting off glossy edges and chrome pillars that support the bar.

Finally, I pull the elastic out of my hair. Bounds of orange hair cascade down my back, sticking to my slightly damp shoulders and nape. *Like the ocean after a storm,* he used to say. I push his words out, willing myself to forget him. Again. I finish up, double-checking all the lights and locks. I step out the back door.

Motorcycle engines rev and approach behind me as I turn my key in the lock.

My heart drops to my stomach. It's such a familiar sound, so mundane, yet each time I hear it, the only thing I think of is *him*.

I expect the grumbling to travel on, but it doesn't.

It gets louder.

I palm the keys in my hand, fitting one between my knuckles.

I turn.

And my heart stutters in my chest.

There's no way.

A lean, dark-clad man parks his motorcycle by the curb and kicks the stand out. He swings his long leg off the back, moving like water—smooth, effortless.

The wind whips around me again—causing the palm trees above me to shuffle nervously. It lifts the scent of *his* cologne, too, and brings it right to me.

No. This can't be happening.

That smell—fir and leather and smoke—brings back so many memories, so much more violently than I expect it to, so quickly. Memories of tasting his lips, slick with liquor, of being tangled in his king-sized bed, of the wind tearing through my hair as he races down highways with me on the back of his bike.

Of *that* bike.

My ex-boyfriend, Corbin, steps off that bike.

My heart full stops. Falters back to life.

Behind him, two more bikers park their bikes but don't approach.

Only him.

Corbin removes his helmet and tucks it under his arm. He doesn't look up 'til he's almost on me. When he does, he stops cold, too.

"What are you doing here?" he asks.

"I *live* here. What are *you* doing here?"

Corbin looks as if something inside him has just shattered. His dark, chestnut eyes search my face. "You *live* here?" he asks in a whisper, voice gravelly and low. His mouth moves in a way I've known for a hundred lifetimes: full lips framed by dark scruff.

My chest squeezes.

"Why didn't you…" his voice, a roll of thunder, "I thought you still…"

My hands feel tacky, my lips dry. I lick them, and the air brushes coldly against my mouth. For a fleeting second, I want *his* breath—his warm breath—on my lips, trickling into my mouth. The stillness in me, my own resolution, surprises me as I finish the words lost to him, "You thought I still lived in Chicago."

Corbin's eyes stop searching my face, my hair, my neckline, and dive straight into my eyes. "How long? Why didn't you tell me?"

"I needed a break, Ben," I say slowly. "I don't *belong* to you. I'm not *yours*."

That word. *Yours*. At the sound of it, Corbin's eyes flare.

"C'mon, Ben!" one of his friends shouts from behind him. "If they're closed, let's just hit the next one."

Corbin steps closer to me, and that's when I smell it—the liquor dripping from all his hard edges. They're barhopping, and this is just one of their stops. This was a total coincidence.

Chapter Three

CORBIN

"Did you know she was here?" Nathan asks as we park our bikes at our next bar.

"Hell no," I say. I make straight for the saloon-style door. My surroundings are an afterthought—the old-style tiled ceiling, the mosaic floor, the rustic mirrors behind the bar that make the room look twice as big. Music cracks in my ears, lyrics inaudible at the volume it's being played.

Nathan leans into my peripheral vision. His wispy blond hair sways with his movements. "Are you sure this whole road trip wasn't just to *run into her?*"

I order the bar's signature drink—Pirate's Punch—then turn away from Nathan.

Beatrix takes my other side and pins me still with her storm-blue eyes. "He makes a good point, Ben."

I back away from the bar, leaving my friends to order their own drinks. Two deep swigs, and I already feel an edge of a buzz returning. All I'm thinking: *I need more. I can't be sober. This trip was supposed to get my mind off her and move on, maybe hook up or meet someone new. She ghosted me for six months. It's over, even if I'm not over her, so it's finally time to get over her.*

I glance around, trying to see if I have a fraction of a chance with anyone in the bar.

Nathan seems to catch on to exactly what I'm trying to do, so he loops his arm in mine and leads me through the loud main room into one of the back rooms of the bar. We weave through jiving, dancing bodies and come to a quieter room that hosts a few, velvet-green pool tables and the clack of resin balls splitting and rolling across the tables.

"Maybe it's meant to be? Maybe she'll come around?" Nathan offers.

"Doubt it," I mutter between another deep swig of burning, pineapple-sweet syrup. My teeth hurt. My head hurts. I would never admit it to Nathan or Bea, but they probably already know this too: My heart hurts worse than it did the day Katrina walked out of my life.

"Play me?" Bea asks as she claims a pool table with a spare quarter.

I shake my head. Another swallow.

I don't want to be awake.

This was supposed to be fun.

I back up to a wall and watch Nathan and Beatrix play a game of pool together. Nathan shows off as much as he can—hopping balls over others and winking at any girl who watches a little too long. Bea, ever the spiteful one, mocks Nathan and winks at the same girls. With her crop top showing off a lethal set of abs, I wouldn't be surprised if she managed to swoon a girl faster than Nathan.

A duo of blonds makes their way into the room from the bar's yard. From the looks of it, a set of siblings. One is a woman who looks to be about our age, with stunning blue eyes and tangled, curly blond hair. Beside her, her brother looks younger and moodier, with his hands stuffed into his pockets and a brooding expression painting his sour features.

They make their way over—to my surprise—to *us*.

The blonde puts a quarter on the pool table with a grin on her face. She leans forward with one hand still resting on the side of the table. "I call next round with you, blue eyes."

Bea looks up and grins back.

"Y'all passing through?" the brother asks.

Between two more sips, I survey the set.

The brother looks at me. "We recognize strangers in this town."

I quirk an eyebrow. "Must be a small town, then…"

"Callie," the blonde sways over to me, hand outstretched. "My brother's name is Rin."

I shake Callie's hand.

"Doubles," Callie offers. "You and me versus your friends."

Regretfully, I let my eyes slide down her figure. I admire her bluntness, her openness. I find looking at her is as easy as watching the sun break over the horizon—her plaid shirt and holey jeans fitting loosely over her girlish figure. I tell myself that Nathan's right—that maybe things played out the way they did for a reason. I know right away, I have to see this…*thing* through with Katrina, but one game of pool isn't going to hurt anyone.

MY HEAD IS SPINNING BY the time my friends and I finally check into our hotel. The hotel is old—I can smell it in the walls—and it sits overlooking the Amelia River. I look out the windows as the three of us trek up to our suite on woozy feet and numb knees. Outside, the moon reflects on the black water below. I make the mistake of glancing up, only to find a huge mural above the spiraling staircase we're currently climbing. Larger-than-life Roman numerals sit around a deep blue circle that depicts the night sky, full of stars. Two steel, black arms click around above us. It triggers a wave of dizziness that makes me grab for the railing.

"For fuck's sake, what's so hard about keeping an elevator running?" Nathan gripes. "You'd think with how many bars there are on this street, enough drunk people would come through. They gotta know stairs are a challenge."

"Give it a break, Nate," Beatrix says.

"God, I'm so drunk," Nate says.

I roll my eyes, but I'm right there with him. After our game of pool, I'd doubled down on the drinks. Shots, beers, anything I could get my hands on. Finally, the bartender cut me off and Nathan and Bea dragged my drunk ass out. We left our bikes parked at a bar two blocks over and trudged our way here.

And I still can't clear my mind. Questions swirl endlessly, just like my surroundings.

What did I do wrong? Was I too much? Was she not in love? Did she know I bought a ring?

My hand finds its way to my chest, where a gold-and-diamond ring hangs from a chain beneath my v-neck tee. I'd been ready to give it to her. We'd gone on a date, *the* date. I was ready to ask when she told me she needed space.

So I gave that to her instead.

Navy blue carpet swims beneath me.

Bea tucks herself under my shoulder and props me up.

I gave her so much space. And she just left.

"Fuck, Ben," Bea whispers. "I'm so sorry."

Did I say that out loud?

Doors blur together before me.

Nathan clicks our key card in the door.

Bea and I stumble in. The room brightens suddenly, and I grimace against the blinding pain. Bea dumps me on the sofa.

My head continues to spin. "I fucking love her."

"You're a mess, Ben," one of them says. I can't tell who's speaking. "Get some sleep."

As if you have to tell me twice.

In two minutes, I've blacked out.

THE NIGHT IS COLD. I booked a rooftop dinner for Katrina. She's always loved the night sky, and ever since I've known her, I have too. She says the deep blue makes her think of an endless ocean. I wonder if that ever meant more than face value, if part of her longed more for the ocean than the night sky. I never asked.

I should have asked.

We're not much for dressing up, so the two of us are in jeans and tees—though she always pulls that off better than I do. Her black pants are skin tight, hugging her dainty ankles and her curvy hips. Her tee is just low enough that I get a glance at the top of her lace bra every time she leans forward just a little too far. It's more than intentional; she's trying to cue me in on what's coming later.

As if she thought I wouldn't take her without the fancy lingerie.

Under my own tee, I have a chain with a ring on it safely tucked away. I didn't trust myself with a box, not ever since I bought the ring a few weeks back. Besides, I wanted the ring close to my heart. It was a promise of forever, after all.

I could see myself in no other outcome than with her, day in and day out, for the rest of my life. Her unruly red hair, her amber eyes that glowed like molten fire in the daylight, the peppering of freckles that patterned her very own starry sky across her skin. I could spend the rest of my life counting each and every freckle on her cheeks, her shoulders, the span between her hip bones.

We sit and our waiter pours some champagne—I've already asked for some preparations before arriving. Maybe that's what tipped her off.

Katrina takes a deep swallow of the alcohol before I can get a word out of my mouth. Her face is clouded, distant. Something is coming.

I already know what's coming.

Ask, I prompt myself. Again. Before it's too late—ask.

I should have asked.

Instead, her petal-pink lips start moving. I can't hear the words, but I can read them: Ben, we need to talk. I love you, but I need some space. I think we should take a break.

The dream shatters.

The night I envisioned: taking the ring from under my collar and holding it up to her eyes, a smile on my own lips. A smirk on hers. She's anything but traditional, anyone but one to settle down. I wouldn't ask her to. Not truly settle down, but stay wild by my side. But maybe a promise of forever was too much of a commitment.

My heart shatters next.

Her lips are moving again. Her voice is silent. Her words are carved on my brain: I'll get a cab home.

She stands.

I stand.

Please don't follow me, Ben.

I WAKE SLOWER THAN I would have expected. Sunlight breaks through the windows, too bright and too loud. I close my eyes, but I'm too awake, too conscious, to slip into another dream to purge the memory I've just relived. Dread washes over me at my next thought.

I followed you anyway, didn't I, Kat?

Chapter Four

KATRINA

Good thing you have the day off, I think to myself. I'm not sure what I would have done if I had to go back to work and face not only my coworkers and act normal—as if my whole life hadn't just been shaken to the core. I'm not sure if I could've faced the risk of seeing Corbin again.

I roll out of bed and rub my face until I get the tired out of my eyes. My bedroom is small, with wood-lined walls that are painted white. Two huge windows flank my bed, and I can see that the sky is only beginning to lighten outside. If I'm quick, I might make it to the sunrise.

With nothing better to do, that's what I decide on. I pull on a pair of jeans and a loose black tee. My heart sinks when I look in the mirror. This is the outfit I wore the last time I saw Corbin in Chicago, the night I decided to leave. But I don't have time to dig through my wardrobe to find anything else comfortable. I grab a blanket off the couch in my small living room then head out the door.

Behind me, the door latches and auto-locks, leaving me on the small, fenced porch. I hurry down a few steps then make my way to the sidewalk. As it is in Florida—as I've been finding—the day is already suffocatingly warm, the air sticky.

My walk to the beach is short—just two roads over. My tired legs wobble on the loose white stone walkways, and I'm grateful to finally reach the sand. It comes with its own challenge, but at least I can ditch my shoes and feel the warmth on my feet. I close my eyes, savor the sensation. I leave my sandals on the top of the wooden boardwalk then look out over the coast. The ocean is crystal blue, the sky its own shade of periwinkle and dashed with orange clouds. The air smells of salt and seawater.

I walk straight to it—each section of the beach is unique in its own way. First, the sand lets my feet sink deep into divots along the ground. Then, it's less powdery. A line of sharp shells crunch beneath my heels. At the waterline, the sand is packed and brown.

The foaming waves crash lazily before me, sizzling along the sand right at my toes. I step forward so that the next wave reaches all the way out towards my feet. The water is warm, but cooler than the air around me.

I close my eyes, and I let everything rush back. The sounds of the waves thundering in and out matches my own breath.

The impression of the ring under Corbin's shirt that night. The way his hands were damp with sweat. The way he smiled nervously, no hint of the crass attitude he could so often have. The dinner. It was too nice. It was too *different,* too unlike Corbin. I knew from the moment he opened the car door for me. Don't get me wrong, it was a nice gesture, but it was never *us.*

I have always been my own person, never his. *Never* his.

That's when it hits me.

I have never belonged to anyone. I've never even belonged to a mother, not a father, not ever a family at all. It was something I never even told Ben—the fact that I grew up in the system, passed from household to household. I never wanted him to know that I was unwanted like that by my true parents—wherever they might be—and by any other couple that tried to raise me.

How could he want me when no one else did?

In the darkness of my mind, I see the families that raised me. I remember one man whose wife passed during the time of my stay with them. I remember how he turned his cold, pale eyes on me and blamed me for her death. I remember the feeling of the backside of his hand on my face, the feeling of my wrists splintering against the floor. I was taken out of that foster home quickly after, but the damage remains done.

How could *he* love *that?*

I open my eyes and stare out over the sea. It rages with the fury in my own soul, pushing and pulling and tossing and turning restlessly at my feet. I feel like I'm staring at a mirror, looking into the depths of my own soul—the drowning insecurities and fears, the way I can never sit still, never *stay* in one place or with any*one* too long. Every few years, I tear my own roots out of the ground and leave the temporary life I've made there. First it was the foster homes, then it was changing cities. First it was the one-night stands with strangers, then it was Corbin. Never stay too long. That way, no one can hurt me. No one can pretend to care. No one can break my heart before I break theirs.

Just like when I left Corbin at the dinner table with an untouched glass of champagne and a ring hiding on the groove of his muscled chest.

He didn't mean it, I tell myself.

A rogue wave crashes at my feet and soaks the folded-up hems of my pants. I gasp at the sensation, but it quickly turns into an uneasy laugh. Then slowly, a real laugh.

Then, an unwarranted thought: *What if you were meant to meet him here? What if this is your chance to tell him?*

I look from my sandy-wet feet back up to the horizon. The sun is breaking over the water—leaving the sky in a wash of bright pinks, yellows, and oranges. The daylight presses a new warmth against my face. I've learned that to be the feeling of *first* daylight, and nothing has come close to matching that sensation. It's bright and it's new.

I stare at the sun for a few seconds, leaving spots in my eyes. Part of me wants to stare until I go blind, because I know, deep down, if there's any chance Corbin sticks around, I won't be able to resist his puppy-dog eyes when he begs.

Chapter Five

CORBIN

I FIND TIME TO TAKE a cold shower after coordinating with Nathan for time in our shared hallway bathroom; it makes me miss my black-and-silver flat back in Chicago—and the privacy that came with it—if only temporarily. I let the water spray on my face, washing away the stickiness of liquor off my lips. I wait until I can feel my whole body again before I wash my hair and scrub my beard. As if I needed another reminder of her, a memory of Katrina hits me.

SHE'S SITTING ON THE BATHROOM counter at my place back in Chicago. She's not wearing much, just a lacy push-up bra and a scrap of fabric that can barely be considered underwear. She beckons me over, a razor blade in her hand. She's done her makeup lethally today—a sharp cat-eye and blood-red lips. She smiles lazily, knowing I'm a sucker for her, that I'll do anything she asks.

I walk to her, and she latches a foot behind my legs, drawing me in closer. With one finger, she pushes my chin up. Her breath tickles my neck. "You need a shave, boy."

I smile. "Want to help?"

SHE ALWAYS DID.

Now, I'll admit, I've let myself go a little. My hair is longer, brushing the tops of my tees and jackets. My beard is unruly, but it gets a monthly overall shave to keep it trim. But every time I try to close shave my neck, I think of her, the thoughts jarring enough to nick myself one too many times.

I rinse off, trying to focus on the water sliding down my chest and back to keep the thoughts at bay. It doesn't help much. I turn off the water, towel off. Knowing shaving would call back one too many more memories, I opt to dress quickly and step away from the bathroom as fast as I can.

"Got any plans today, boss? Or are we still checking out tonight?" Nathan asks from his hotel bed. He has a phone in hand, scrolling mindlessly.

Beatrix is perched on the corner of her made bed. She looks at me expectantly, her sharp features cracking with a knowing grin. Her short black hair is still in wet spikes from her own shower. "My money's on staying at *least* one more night. If not more," she says slyly. "I mean, why not? It's a cute little town."

I roll my eyes and pocket my phone in my jeans. "I was going to see about extending our reservation…"

Nathan cackles.

I shoot him a glare.

"Our man's got it bad, Bea," he says, wiggling his eyebrows.

"Nothing we didn't already know," Beatrix says.

"Hey, why didn't we ever meet her?" Nathan asks.

"She's pretty reserved," I say.

"*Buuulll,*" Nathan drawls. "No way. That girl's fucking wild as a storm. I could see it in her eyes."

I can't disagree. It was one thing we had painfully in common: wild blood. Neither of us wanted much safety, from a relationship, from life. So what changed her? *What am I missing?*

"Why did you guys break up again?" Bea asks.

I don't answer right away. How can I even tell them? I'm mortified. I'm not even sure, myself. So I say the only thing I can muster, the words she told me, the cheap excuse. "She said she needed a break."

Nathan's eyebrows hit his hairline. "Then moves to fucking *Florida?* Why didn't she tell you?"

"That's what I said…" I mutter.

"Aw, dude, you gotta see this through."

A mirror to my own thoughts. *I know. I know.* That's why Nathan's always been my best friend; he can voice what's in my head, as if he knows me better than he knows himself.

"Let's go back to the diner," Bea offers.

"I want to go on my own."

Bea shrugs. "Suit yourself. We're here if you need us."

I check the diner's hours on my phone before heading out. Since our hotel is right on the water, too, it's a short three-minute walk—through the parking lot and over a railroad—to the marina and the diner. The dock lines the water then curves around the restaurant, where it perches out on the edge with a one-eighty view of the water around it. I climb a few wooden steps up to the wrap-around porch to the diner's front door.

I push the door open to be greeted with a mostly empty room. A few people sit around, eating hash browns and scrambled eggs. My mouth waters at the smells, and I suddenly regret that I skipped out on breakfast to come here.

Though, as much as I search the floor and the staff coming in and out of the kitchen, I don't find Katrina.

"How many?" a young server asks me.

"Just one."

"Make that two," a sweet voice says behind me.

I glance over my shoulder to see Callie walking in.

"Unless, of course, you'd rather eat alone," she says.

I shake my head.

The server walks us over to the bar, and we sit on stools at the counter and glance over the menus in an awkward silence.

"Day drinks?" she asks.

"I'm not above it," I say. *Especially after last night.*

"Good. I need a little hair of the dog, if you know what I mean. They have a killer Bloody Mary."

My nose wrinkles involuntarily.

"If that's not your style, try the Pineapple Martini." Callie points to my drink menu. Her nails are unpainted and short.

I take her word for it and order our drinks. I think back to the night before; I can't remember exactly the moment we parted ways. The night is flashes of her curly blond hair and moments of delirium when I thought maybe Katrina was the one there instead, leaning across the pool table with her hips too close to mine. I remember touching the small of her back, calling Katrina's name. Callie's confusion, Bea's smooth cover-up, Nathan calling it a night.

I wonder if she remembers it at all.

"So, tell me." Callie turns her body towards mine. Her pale knees poke through the torn fabric of her blue jeans. "What made a bad boy like you blow into town?"

With her full attention pinned on me, I find it hard to swallow. I rub a hand over the scruff on my face, hold it there. "My friends and I are road-tripping cross-country," I say.

"Are you staying a while?" Her blue eyes flicker across my face, landing on my knuckles, my lips, then my eyes.

I pause. "Yes."

Callie smiles, and the room warms a few degrees. "My dad has a couple rentals on the island. I could hook you up. It'll be cheaper than staying in a hotel."

I nod, still struggling over the cotton in my throat. Our drinks arrive, and I take a swallow immediately. The taste is similar to the punch from the night before, but this is more bitter, sharper, like true pineapple. My mouth waters at the flavor. *Thank God.*

Callie offers me a card.

I take it warily, and my fingers brush the soft tips of hers.

"This is my dad's realtor card. When you call, tell him I sent you."

I nod. "Thank you."

"Anytime," she says, smiling with perfect, straight white teeth.

It's clear to me now—she comes from money. Island money, so it seems, and it doesn't surprise me. Drinks the morning after a night out; nothing screams *money* more. I know from my own experience; my own pockets are lined with my father's money, and my friends know it. Sadly, my father's currently funding a high-functioning alcoholic. Maybe in both our situations.

I order myself a plate of brunch and offer to buy Callie some food too, but she turns it down.

Something about Callie sitting patiently in our silence makes me want to trust her, to confide in her, but I'm not stupid enough to gush about girl problems in front of a girl who blatantly shows interest. *Why not see* this *through?* The thought runs across my mind, as if it might be scared I'll chase after it for even proposing the possibility. But instead, I chase it in a different way, watching Callie under a new light. I did find Katrina here, and that might mean something, but if Katrina wanted space from me so badly, surely she wouldn't care if I found someone new.

"How long have you lived here?" I ask.

"All my life," Callie says. "My parents raised me and my siblings on a farm out in Callahan. They own properties out here, too, and they let us stay where we want. Can't complain." She raises her Bloody Mary in a mock cheers to her parents. The rim of the cup is loaded with celery, garnish, and a fat shrimp.

"What do you do for work?"

Callie laughs.

I raise my eyebrows and take a deep drink. The buzz sets in, starting at my fingertips and toes. The next drink hits my knees. I shovel more salt-and-pepper hash browns in my mouth to counteract the alcohol. Who knows what I might do if I get too drunk the second time around.

"I'm *joking*," she says finally, though I know she's clearly not. She pops the shrimp in her mouth and chews thoughtfully. "I volunteer at the humane society. I love animals, so it's a nice pastime. What do *you* do for work?"

Annnddd now it's my turn to be humiliated.

"Surely it's not easy to just drop everything and drive cross-country on motorcycles with your friends."

"You got me, miss money bags," I mutter. "My dad owns a pharmaceutical company up in Chicago. My kid's kids are set for life."

"You got kids?"

"Not yet," I mumble into the rim of my glass.

"Plans?"

I think about Katrina. I think about the last time we had sex, how she was nervous—despite her birth control—to get pregnant. I think about the way, if she were to ever get pregnant, I would cut the hands off of anyone who would even consider looking at her too long. I think too, about the way her eyes look after we've finished.

I take a swig of my martini. "Maybe with the right person," I catch myself saying, when in reality, it means *maybe with her.*

KATRINA

I WRONGFULLY THINK I'M IN the clear two days later when I show up for my afternoon closing shift.

Jackson finds me as soon as I walk into the diner and asks if we can talk outside.

I nod numbly, confused.

Jackson walks me out of the diner to the head of the dock. The tables seated outside are mostly empty right now, but we both know as dinner draws closer, the diner will fill quickly. I look out over the water, studying the small fishing boats and the single million-dollar yacht that sticks out like a sore thumb on the docks. The air is thick with the smell of fish and seawater. Thank God for the shade, otherwise I think I might melt away under the combined heat of the sun and Jackson's attention.

"How are you today?" Jackson starts casually—a telltale sign this conversation is going to be a lot more serious than I want it to be.

"I'm…" Fine? No. Alright? Barely. I came here to escape, and my past chased me down. "I've got some personal things going on," I settle on finally.

"Do those personal things have anything to do with a dark-haired biker who's been loitering around the restaurant?" Jackson asks.

I close my eyes and curse inwardly. "Maybe."

"He's been getting breakfast here, looking around like he's *looking* for something or someone. Yesterday he asked about you."

"I'm gonna kick his ass," I mutter. I step away from Jackson and move to the edge of the raised dock. People walk by on the dock below, making their way to afternoon tours on boats or catamarans. I listen to the vague chatter of tourists and locals alike; I wonder if I still fall into the tourist category, or if now—after three months of living here—I might be a new local. I'm sure Corbin still qualifies as a tourist. I wonder if that will ever change…

"Is he giving you trouble? The sheriff's office…"

"No," I say quietly. "He's my ex from up north. We were pretty serious then. I don't think he planned to run into me here. He didn't even know I moved here."

Jackson is silent for a moment.

"I'm safe, I promise."

"I know it's none of my business, but…" Jackson walks to my side and leans on the edge of the dock. "Do you still love him?"

I don't answer. Somewhere inside me, a small voice says, *You've loved him since the moment you laid eyes on him, and you'll love him in every life after this one.*

Jackson watches me; I can see it in my periphery. "I'm here for you if you need anything."

"Thank you, Jackson," I say.

"Anytime," Jackson says. He gives me a short pat on the shoulder, then heads back in.

I take a moment to regain my composure. Seagulls call overhead. Wind rustles in the palm trees around the diner. A kid screams with delight somewhere to my right. Looking over, I see a child pointing at a group of pelicans sitting atop wooden pilings that rise from the water. It's a view you see often here—if not on the water like what's before me now, then in each and every gallery that all the retirees use as hobby-central. I miss the larger-than-life murals from my city life for a moment, painted bodies with flower blooms for heads or birds painted with whorls of neon. The art here seems less of creativity and more of mimicry—fine in its own right, but more boring to me than I expected. I want to see art that makes me stir inwardly, art that makes me feel the anger and sadness I hold inside me. I want to feel *seen* in art for all my internal struggles.

This town, small as it is, is lonelier than I thought it would be.

JACKSON AND I CLOSE THE DINER together. We part ways after we lock up the back door, and I walk to my car, grateful to be done. Loose gravel crunches under my heels. Then I hear loose gravel under someone else's shoes too, dead ahead. I look up.

Black biker boots.

Connected to long, lanky legs.

Which meet that narrow waist and wide shoulders.

Fuck me, he's always had that golden ratio of a body. I stop before I reach him.

Corbin is leaning back against my car, muscled arms crossed. He's ditched his leather jacket tonight, leaving his white tee visible. It stretches across his shoulders, his chest.

I look away, fighting to swallow the emotions rising to the surface. I glance back for Jackson, but he's already driving off.

"Your boss didn't even make sure you made it to your car alright?" Corbin asks, his voice like smoke.

I walk around him to the other side of my car, open the driver's door, and toss my stuff in. "This town is safe. It's an honest mistake."

Corbin is behind me suddenly, one hand on the roof of my car and the other on my door. His breath smells like cinnamon, and I can't tell if it's gum or whiskey as it spills warmly over my shoulder and neck.

I turn to look up at him. I expect some snarky remark, some borderline argument statement that begs me to fight. We've always been weak for it, the strife that comes with our relationship, walking the edge of a conversation that's one push away from being heated. But he only looks at me with confusion and pain all over his face, all in his deep brown eyes. I lose myself to it, the crease at the side of his lip, the way the two freckles on his left cheek pinch with his narrowed eyes. His lips are chapped, just a little bit. His crooked teeth, peeking out, just a little bit.

"Why didn't you tell me you moved, Kat?" His voice is like the wind, breathy, weak. For now. "I was going to ask you to *marry me*."

There it is. The words hanging between us, the words we were both too scared to say out loud.

"Fuck, Katrina, I was *so* in love with you."

"Was?" I ask. I curse myself for even caring, for considering as his eyes drill into me that maybe he doesn't still feel the way he did then, now.

He sees his mistake, his darkened eyes on my mouth, then my eyes. "I would stop the world from spinning if it meant I could keep you in my arms."

My chest squeezes again. Hard. I struggle to breathe. It was always these little things—the way he said words like this—that stole the air from my lungs time and time again. The conviction in his eyes. The way his hands flex, like he's two seconds away from acting on his words. Pure devotion. I would know.

I try to duck into my car, but he stops me with a hand around my arm.

Electricity bounces through me. His hand wraps all the way around my arm, his chewed fingernails side-by-side. A tiny sign of weakness, invisible unless you look close enough. Stress. Worry. Insecurity. He has everything he could dream of—money, friends, fun—but he doesn't have me. "Give me one more chance, Katrina," he begs. "Maybe it was Chicago. Maybe there was too much going on there. Maybe here we can try again."

Maybe it's because you can't tell him the truth about yourself, I think.

I almost pull away. Almost.

But his cologne is overpowering, reminding me too much of our late nights, the sheets a mess and sweat covering our bodies. The sounds of our sighs.

"Let's go for a ride," he says. His face is inches from mine, and I can feel his breath on my lips.

I turn my head to search for his bike and find it parked a few spots over. It used to be a weekend thing, driving around the city at night. I would be lying to myself if I said I didn't miss it—the thrill, the adrenaline, holding onto his body for dear life. My only regret is not having purchased my own motorcycle during the duration of our relationship.

Corbin leans in, and his lips brush the arch of my ear.

I shiver at the sensation.

"I'll bring you back home whenever you're ready," he murmurs the words against the top of my ear.

It's a taunt. He knows what it'll turn into. I know what it'll turn into, too. We're reliving our first few months of dating. I refused him, over and over again. Yet, he pursued. The night always ended in sex. The morning always ended with me sneaking out before he could beg me to stay. Because as soon as he has a moment to beg, I'm in his hands. He can use me however he wants.

"Okay," I whisper.

Warily, his hand loosens on my arm, and his fingertips trail down the length of my arm, sending another shiver through me. His fingers brush the side of my hand, the edge of my palm. I want to give in. I want to take his hand.

His touch sends currents through my blood.

I don't pull away when he rubs his fingers across my palm carefully, as he pulls me forward with just enough strength to convince me. I find myself closing my car door, locking it, then letting his hand wrap around mine fully, letting him lead me to his motorcycle.

The world moves around me. My body moves of its own accord. I'm officially out of my own control, wrapped in the spell Corbin's placed on me. He straddles his motorcycle, and I take in the sight of the metal beast before I follow suit—glossy, midnight-black covers the frame. From a distance, I hadn't even noticed his bike is newer than the one he had when I saw him last. The model is the same; no doubt he traded it in for the latest year. This one looks sleeker, faster. The wheels and brand decal are all blacked out, but I know Corbin has always had a preference on bikes, so I guess at the brand. Ducati. Expensive. Fast as hell. Dangerous, like him.

Corbin offers me his helmet.

I want to take it and toss it, just to show him if he's not above wearing a helmet then neither am I, but I'm pulled in by his eyes again, his voice as he says, "Put it on, Kat." His voice thrums through me. He could ask anything—*anything*—tonight.

I take the black helmet and put it over my head. It makes my curls cling tight around my neck, and it smells like *him*. The heady scent of leather and fir and spice. My stomach somersaults inside me. I straddle the motorcycle behind him.

You know this is the point of no return, I think to myself. *You do this, you're a goner.*

Corbin kicks the motorcycle to life. The machine sways and purrs beneath me, making my nerves jolt. After six months, I'm surprised to find it's making me anxious to be on the back of his motorcycle again. "Hold tight, Kat," Corbin rumbles.

I wrap my arms around his middle, finding he's just as toned and firm as he was before. My heart hurts a little at the thought. I wonder if he's hooked up to get his mind off *us*. I haven't; not yet, at least. I've tried, with plenty of tipsy nights at the Sandbar & Kitchen, but most ended up alone, lying flat on the sand and staring up at the stars. Most nights, I just think of him. Of the night he took me to that rooftop dinner under the stars. The way he *knew* me like that, so well. He knows me so well.

Chapter Seven

CORBIN

I THOUGHT I WAS READY to have her back on my bike, but I guess my body thinks otherwise. Butterflies assault my stomach, making it twist and turn inside me. Every simple movement of the bike that I know so well becomes the Olympic Games. I try to hold steady and not jerk my motorcycle around too much as I navigate out of the parking lot and away from Katrina's rose-gold Lexus. Something inside me is a little surprised she still drives the car I bought her for her twenty-seventh birthday a year back. After her whole up-and-leaving stint, I figured she'd want nothing at all to do with me. Still, a car is a car…

Katrina's arms tighten around my middle; I hear her let out a short breath, a short gasp follows. Her heart pounds against my back.

"Tell me where to go," I say to her. It surprises me how easy her responses come, how hypnotized she seems to be by just my voice. "Show me a spot only the locals know."

"Okay," she says, her voice muffled by my helmet. "Take this road down to Fletcher. When you hit the beach, turn right."

I nod and lift my black bandanna over my nose. We cruise down Centre Street slowly. The quaint, 1800s-style shops on either side of the road are all closed up by now, save the bookstore on our right. All along the street, live oaks twist and spiral over the road, wrapped with golden Christmas lights. The air is humid and sweet, and I catch a lingering whiff of chocolate fudge as we ride.

I wish we were still in love.

We get lucky with a green light, and I lift my foot to change gears. The streets open up a little, leaving wide fields with cozy parks and tennis courts and school buildings. The live oaks wander down this way too, continuing to flank us at odd spots along the way. The scenery is so different from Chicago and the north. In all my free time, I regret to say that Florida was never much of an interest of mine, so it never made the road trip pit-stops Nathan and Beatrix and I made. However, as all our other road trip routes were too similar, my two friends were convinced I needed something new to get my mind off Katrina, something more extreme. Our final destination was supposed to be Miami, and we planned to party for a week straight there, no sleep. So how I find myself cruising down a thirty-five mile-per-hour road in the middle of a small beach town baffles me. I was ready for booze every night, maybe even some designer drugs while we were at it.

Katrina's dainty hands clutch at my stomach as I speed over a small hill ahead of us. As we breach the top, I'm greeted with a vast scene of the marshes and a creek that runs through the middle. In the dwindling evening, it's painted with lilac purples and hazy pinks. It's *beautiful*.

"This is Egan's Creek," she half-mumbles, half-yells to me over the noise of the wind and my engine. I can barely hear her.

I just nod.

When we reach the next light, I find we're right at the edge of the island; the sea is visible just over the parking lot on the other side of the light. Overhead, a full moon rises in the pink and purple sky, sending shimmers over the stirring ocean water.

Katrina taps my right bicep—a signal we used to use when she would guide me to places she wanted to go back when we were dating—and the sudden surge of familiarity sends a rush of excitement through me. *You're still in here. You're still the girl I love.*

"Hold tight," I warn Katrina as the light turns green.

She tightens her arms around me.

I push the throttle and gun it down the road. Wind lashes my hair from my face, roars in my ears. We race past multi-million-dollar houses that line the road on either side. I wonder, too, why my father never bought a beach house with all the money he had. Maybe our family was just more suited to the cold.

I wonder what Katrina is more suited to. The cold? Or this? The way the salty-sticky air leaves a layer of silt on my skin. The way, even though the sun has set, the land still pulses with heat. The way time seems to stand still. Deep down, I know it feels more like her. In those ways and so many more. She was always the more adventurous one. While I could ride for hours, she was the one who wanted to jump in Lake Michigan at the Indiana Beaches. I couldn't imagine driving all the way back home with dirty, wet feet stuck back into soggy socks and leather boots; the idea of trying to shake the lake water out of my hair and still tasting it when I licked my own lips. It didn't ever appeal to me. But I can see her true nature here— I can see her jumping into the ocean with hair like the rays of the sun itself. I see her basking in the seawater glow—tacky skin, tangled hair, sandy toes. It does feel like her.

I weave through a roundabout then gun it again.

As we drive, the road slopes ever so slightly down and around to the right. Houses all around get bigger with every passing mile, astonishing me. Money in Chicago looks different than money in Florida.

We stop at a red light, and I feel Katrina heave a breath behind me.

"Don't tell me you're scared?" I tease. I flex lightly under her desperate grasp.

Katrina shakes her head fervently. "It's just been a while. It's a rush…adrenaline," she mutters.

"Where am I going?"

"Take this left. It's the scenic route. Canopy Road," she tells me.

I follow her lead.

The trees reach over us suddenly, enveloping us in a tunnel of rustling leaves, I find myself weaving one way then the other, twisting through the winding road. I've seen roads like this in Tennessee, but never with live oaks this massive blotting out the sky from view. With the oncoming dusk, it almost feels as if we're driving through a cave.

Katrina taps my left bicep as we approach a bisecting road. It hits me now more than ever—with the trickle of traffic that's slowing with every passing minute—how much of a small town this really is. "Left here. Then we're straight for a while. I'll tap you again before we turn into the park," she says.

When it's clear, I pull out and accelerate down the road. Aside from a few roundabouts, I'm able to speed down this length of road pretty quickly. Trees race in my periphery. Before I know it, the road lets out onto a bridge, and the sound *whirs* in my ears. A few moments later, Katrina taps once, a sign to slow down. Two more taps, and I see the sign. I pull into the park entrance to be met with a closed wooden gate.

Katrina pulls my helmet off her head. "Go around," she tells me.

I maneuver my bike around the far side of the gate. Part of me wants to ask if she thinks we'll get caught, but at the end of the day, I don't really care. The worst damage they can do is possibly fine us. I park my motorcycle at the far end of the lot, tucked behind a hedge for good measure.

Katrina steps off my bike and holds the helmet in front of her.

I follow suit, take the helmet, then place it on her seat. "So this is the locals' secret spot?"

Katrina shrugs with one shoulder. "I mean it's a little out of the way and off-island, so I don't know if I would consider it that. But this is my favorite beach."

"Anything like Indiana's beaches?" I ask with a chuckle.

"Way better. Just wait 'til you see," she says. "It's a bit of a hike."

"That gives us time to catch up, then."

Katrina makes a queasy face. She doesn't say anything else but instead starts toward a small break in the tree line.

I follow her then match her stride. "We can start with when you left."

Chapter Eight

KATRINA

I WINCE. OF COURSE. OF course he would want to know that. *How do you tell him you left the night he tried to propose? That you were so suffocated by the pressure of being a good girlfriend, of the mystery of how he could want you when no one else did? How do you lead with that?*

I rack my mind for a date instead. "February seventh," I say.

Corbin stops walking, his feet stop crunching over the gravel and sticks and sand.

You may as well have said, "The day you tried to propose."

I ignore him, and my thoughts, and keep walking. Finally, I hear him catch back up to me.

"Our anniversary."

"And the day we broke up."

Corbin walks silently for a while.

Trees and palm fronds *whoosh* overhead. I focus on the sandy ground as we weave our way around the path I know so well. Below my feet, hazardous branches and stumps are dashed with yellow paint. It feels like our conversation; the things we don't say out loud are only *just* obvious enough to notice and avoid.

"So you just got in your car and drove?" he asks.

I swallow the emotion rising in my throat. "More or less," I whisper. "I packed a bag and left. After I got here, I found a long-term rental and a job and settled in. Then I went back to move my things down."

"I stopped by your place about a month…*after*," he says, and I know what he means. *After our dinner. After his failed proposal.*

"You never called," I say numbly. Honestly, I expected him to. I expected my phone to buzz from the moment I left until I finally caved and picked it up, but no. That dug at me too, deep into that insecurity, into what he *doesn't* know. It felt like he didn't want me, just like it felt like my real parents and foster parents didn't want me.

After a moment, Corbin says, "I was too scared to."

We reach a small hill, and once we climb to the top, the sand slopes away into the beach below us. I stumble down into the moonlit clearing and listen for Corbin's following footsteps.

I don't wait for him. I ditch my shoes and make straight for the water's edge until I can feel the waves tickling the tips of my toes. The smell of salt fills my lungs. I gaze at the incredible sight. All along the beach, old trees protrude from the flat sand, tall, crooked branches and sideways roots reaching out of the ground. All sun-bleached like bones.

"I was scared if I was too overbearing I would drive you away," Corbin says from right beside me.

It makes my heart jump in my chest. He's always been that way—he's always *moved* so silently, like a shadow or an oncoming storm that you didn't expect until the thunder crashed right overhead.

"Sounds like I did that anyway, didn't I?" his voice, a whisper.

I watch the small waves at my feet. My toenails are painted a light blue, the color of the sky. I've never been much for painting nails or anything too feminine like that, but recently I've given in to treating myself. It felt good to feel a little pampered. It was such a change too, from trying to keep up with Corbin and his rough lifestyle, with street racing and drinking and blowing through money like it was leaves in the rain. There was no more betting for the thrill of it in my life, there was only deliberate spending on little things that made me feel more in the moment. Painted nails, beachy maxi dresses, and occasionally a bottomless mimosa at the Florida House Inn for brunch. Some parts of my old life, I could reconsider. I would still buy a motorcycle; here on the island, it would be fun. I could get used to riding around the small-town streets with my hair spiraling in the wind.

Corbin stays silent beside me, ever the patient one to wait for my answers to come around.

"It felt like you didn't care," I admit finally. "You let me walk out of your life, and you didn't even put up a fight." I rub my lips together, fighting a rising tide of emotion. "It felt like you didn't want me."

Corbin runs a hand over his face, the scruff around his mouth, then both his hands brush his wild mane of hair back. "Damn it, Kat, I want you more than anything," he growls the words. "I should have said that then, I realize that now. I just—I… I didn't want you to feel like I was trying to tie you down."

I look at him finally.

He peers deep back into my eyes, his brown eyes pits of darkness in the young evening. His gaze consumes me completely, and I'm taken back to all the memories that I fought so hard to bury—first meeting him and looking up at him just like this, the feeling of our first hug and the way he perched his chin right atop my head, making me feel small and safe in his strong arms. I see him too, in the moments of our silent solace in one another. Fingertips brushing skin, chills pricking my arms. He has always been unpredictable in many ways—much like the weather. But one thing never changes about him: his passion rages like a summer storm, and I always get carried away in the heat of it.

"I was right, then… You felt like I was going to tie you down," he guesses. His rough voice sends chills along my skin again, like a sudden drop in temperature. His features change ever so slightly; a shadow passes over his eyes.

"It's the metaphorical tying down I don't like," I say lowly. A smile plays at my lips at his words, and at my reaction, his face changes again.

A flicker of recognition for his own words, and a flaming blush on his cheeks.

"Isn't that what getting married *is?*" I ask.

Corbin doesn't answer.

"Could you love me if we never married?" Part of me considers my own proposal for a fraction of a moment. If he says yes, will I consider him again?

"What makes you think I would *tie* you down in a marriage?" he snaps. "I wouldn't be taking your freedom, Kat. All I want…" His eyes go distant again. "All I want is to love you, to be able to love you forever."

How can he want you? I grit my teeth at the thought. "Walk with me?" I ask to get out from under his heavy eyes.

Corbin nods, a stifled exhale staggering out of his chest.

I walk the tide line and duck under a few winding, bone-white branches.

"Let's make a bet," Corbin says from behind me.

I come face to face with the bottom root system of a downed tree. I turn, and Corbin is already close behind me. He steps forward without hesitation, pushing me into a divot of the roots. With one hand, he grabs ahold of a root; the other, he plants beside my neck. I'm caged. He always knew it made my heart race, and it does the same now. A kickstart of adrenaline.

Corbin leans in.

He blends in with the night sky behind him so well, save for the twinkle in his eye. He always did come alive at night. "Give me a second chance. Let me prove to you that I'm not tying you down. Let me show you that if we were married, you could still be just as wild."

"And if I win the bet?" I ask. "If it turns out, I can't be?"

"I'll go back to Chicago." Corbin is so close now that I can taste his breath. "But if I win…"

I know exactly what he'll ask, and it makes a hole in my stomach.

"I get to propose."

"Do I have to say yes?" I lean back into the roots.

Corbin leans a little closer, shaking his head. "But you'll want to," he whispers in my ear.

Electricity shoots down my neck and limbs. I close my eyes and bite my cheek to try to stifle the feeling. "You're pretty confident in yourself," I say, but my voice cracks and my face heats, and I can't bring myself to look back at him.

"And you're pretty flustered over, what, not even a kiss?" Corbin teases. His lips brush my ear, and something inside me melts like wax.

I put a hand on his chest to push him away, but find that my muscles arc what's been melted, and I'm left feeling his strong chest and his heart racing beneath his tight tee. *Fuck.*

"Tell me you don't miss me."

"I don't miss you," I lie.

"You're a bad liar, Kat." Corbin presses a small kiss just below my ear, and my nerves turn to liquid fire. "I'll make you one more bet. Kiss me, and if you still think you can say you don't miss me, I'll let you go home alone."

"And if I can't?" My voice is nothing more than the air itself.

"I get to take you home instead."

I look up at the moon and curse inwardly. "I can still lie," I tell him.

"I know you won't, though." Corbin looks at me. His eyes are so intense, his mouth so close to mine. "Kiss me, Katrina," he says, as if he knows to his core that I will do anything he says. Because I will.

He lets me close the distance. He lets *me* initiate. At first touch, his soft lips brush lightly over mine, warm breath heating our skin. Our lips fit perfectly together. My insides flutter. His hands don't move from the branches. He's giving me control. He has me where he wants me, but he won't do anything more than put pressure on my weak ego until it breaks. Corbin's lips open just enough for me to deepen the kiss and lean into it. My hand moves on its own accord, sliding up his chest and neck to tangle in his hair.

Corbin's hands move finally, too. One stays braced on the tree, and the other wraps tightly around the small of my back. All at once, he comes back full force in my memories, replaying in real-time. The way he moves, his arms rigid as if he's trying to hold onto a remaining scrap of sanity; the way he smells like whiskey and fire; the way he tastes like cinnamon and sin.

The kiss stirs us both—hands roving, hair tousling, blood rushing. When our lips part, he's panting, and I can't catch my breath.

"Tell me, Katrina," his voice sounds like a purr.

"I miss you," I whimper. "I miss you more than anything." The truth slips out. If it's true—if he wants me like he says he does—then he's the only one who ever has. But *is* he telling me the truth, and how could I possibly know? How can I know for sure?

Corbin smiles wickedly in the dark.

He has everything. He could have anyone. Why does he want you?

Ever the gentleman in disguise, he asks, "Can I take you home, Katrina?"

I nod, helpless.

Chapter Nine

CORBIN

I WANT TO TAKE HER right here and now. Her face and the skin showing just above her shirt are flushed with red. Her eyes, in the low light of the moon, are fully dilated. Wholly dark. None of her usual golden brown is visible in her iris; she looks feral, wild.

"Where do you want to go?" I ask. I want her to tell me that we're going to stay right here, that she's going to push me into the sand and ride me 'til everything that's happened between us is wiped from our minds.

"There's a place in Jacksonville," she utters. "It's a bit of a ride from here, but it's worth seeing. They have a great spiked lemonade there."

"A hotel?"

"I'm not ready to take you back to my place quite yet," she says, licking her lips.

I gaze at the petal pink of her soft lips, wondering if I could sneak one more kiss in, or if she would push me away and call all the games off. She's always been a sucker for me teasing and pulling her in with fickle bets between the two of us, but we're on unsteady ground, and I'm not sure how much she'll tolerate. "So you're treating me like a one-night stand instead?" I ask.

"And if I am?" Her eyes gleam in the darkness.

I'd give myself to you anyway. That's what I think. What I say is, "You'll want more than one night."

"No strings attached then," she says. She ducks under my arm and starts back for the tree line.

"There are strings attached. We have an active bet, Kat." I follow her. The sand divots beneath my black leather boots.

"That doesn't mean we can't have meaningless sex."

My eyebrows raise on their own. *Meaningless?* I try to wrap my head around what she's said as she moves across the sand. My thoughts quickly change to the amount of speed she has while I struggle behind her. It's clear that she's spent plenty of time on the beach since she moved, and I guess six months is long enough to make this new terrain easy on her.

How can you think sex is meaningless? The thought buzzes around in my head. I've never been one to believe in that notion. Maybe that's what essential difference Katrina and I had. Even in all my past relationships, I could never jump into bed with any of them; there always had to be some sort of established relationship, some sort of emotional connection. Maybe it's to blame on the way I was raised. Everything is meaningless when you have money; everything is replaceable, upgradeable. In that life, back in Chicago, in the social group I had, where everyone had money, even love was replaceable and meaningless. Plenty of my friends had one-night stands when I left the bars to go home alone. I never felt like I was missing out; it was just a piece of me I didn't want to share like that.

"Is our sex meaningless to you?" I ask Katrina as we hike our way back on the trail.

"It's just sex," is her cold response.

"If you say so." I match her short stride with ease and glance down at her. She doesn't look at me, but I can feel the palpable frustration radiating off of her. Her wily hair bounces as she stomps down the trail, and I have to stifle a laugh. *You always did fight me, tooth and nail, Kat.*

We walk in silence until we reach my bike.

"Do you remember the first time we met?" I ask her as she fits my helmet back over her head, a scowl on her face. "You turned me down."

"You paid for my drinks when I didn't ask you to."

"I was trying to be nice," I say.

"I'm a grown woman," she bites back. "I don't need you to look after me."

"But I *wanted* to."

"What the hell, Corbin. Get on the bike."

I do as she says, and she climbs onto the bike behind me.

"Turn left out of the park, and I'll guide you the rest of the way."

I nod then tie my bandanna back around my neck and lift it over my nose. "Hold on tight."

Katrina grabs my middle.

As soon as we're back on the road, my mind wanders back to that first night.

IT'S THE FIRST TIME I'VE been at the bar in a while. When I first turned twenty-one, I lived it up every night, but in the past few years, I've cut back on the drinking. Tonight's the exception. It's my birthday and I wanted to go out, so I did, and now here I am.

The bar is an upscale club, with glass-mirror walls and colorful lasers shooting around for lighting. The bar itself is at the far end of the room, right in front of a massive wall of glass bottles that reaches all the way to the ceiling. A rolling ladder hangs from one of the shelves.

I make my way over and order myself whiskey on the rocks.

Beside me, there's a young woman who's ordering her own drink. A Dirty Shirley. I can smell her perfume from where I stand. When the bartender returns to us, I pick up her tab.

The woman turns to me. Her eyes are honey and fire in the vibrant club lighting. Her face is scattered with orange freckles, and her orange-blond hair tumbles down her shoulders like the ocean at dawn. She's breathtaking. She quirks a rounded eyebrow at me. "Do I look like I can't afford my own drinks?" she asks.

I take my time checking her out—noting a pearl necklace on her collarbones. She wears a tight red dress with one sleeve. The fabric cuts off right above her freckled knees. On her feet, she's wearing a set of painful-looking black stilettos. I wonder exactly how short she'd be without them, and it makes some primal instinct inside me smug. She'd be tiny.

"I never said that. I just wanted your attention."

"You got it. Happy?"

I quirk an eyebrow back at her. "Mostly."

"What's your name, handsome?" she asks, her voice deadpan.

"Corbin, but my friends call me Ben."

"I'm Katrina." She holds her hand out in front of her.

I take her hand and shake it.

She leans in a little and grins at me, all teeth. "You here alone?"

I grin back. "Not anymore."

"I'll entertain this, but I'm not going home with you."

"I never asked you to," I say. I can't help but love her feisty attitude. "Maybe one day."

"Unlikely."

A TAP ON MY CHEST brings me back. We pull onto the interstate, and I gun it. I think of all the ways I could've stopped her from walking out of my life, of all the things I did wrong. I lose myself for a moment, spiraling into a deathtrap of emotions. I should have called. I should have slept on her doormat until I realized she'd gone. I should have looked for her. I should have chased her here, not rolled up six months later ready to fuck my way through my feelings.

Katrina tightens her grip as I speed down the interstate.

My heart races at the feeling.

I'm not sure what waits for us at the hotel, if that's another fight or her pulling back into her shell and shutting me out, or if it's a drunk affair that I'm walking into blindly. It doesn't really matter, because either way I'm willing to see it through. I'm ready to fight her until her walls break in half. I always knew there was more that she wasn't sharing; I can tell she *still* hasn't shared those secrets yet.

Katrina guides me off the interstate and along a road that flanks the sea. We pull into a parking lot made of cobblestone and Katrina points at a small lot in front of a hotel called the Seahorse Oceanside Inn. "Their bar is around back," she says.

I park my motorcycle, and we walk up to the hotel check-in. Sliding doors *whir* open and ice-cold AC rushes out, washing the humidity off of me. The small room is white and it smells like the inside of a refrigerator. We book one room, with one bed, claim our key, then step back out into the clammy night.

"They have a pool, too," Katrina says.

"*We* don't have swimsuits," I tell her.

Katrina shrugs and shimmies off towards the room.

I follow her, eyebrows creased. *Surely she doesn't mean…*

We walk up an outdoor flight of stairs and walk through a dark, damp hallway to the other side of the hotel. The balcony opens up to a view of the blue-lit pool and a small bar tucked in the far right corner of the downstairs landing. The ocean is somewhere in the darkness beyond.

Katrina finds our room number and slides our key into the metal lock. It clicks and beeps and the door unlatches. We walk inside.

The first thing Katrina does is shut the freezing AC off.

I flick on a light.

"Want to order takeout?" she asks.

"Dinner and a date, huh?"

"Lucky you." Katrina lifts her shirt over her head and turns to lock her sights on me.

My breath hitches in my chest.

Her pants hit the ground next, and I'm left staring at the set of lacy red scraps she calls underwear. I step forward, but she puts her hand out and clicks her tongue.

"Ditch the shirt," she tells me.

My stomach bottoms out. Slowly, I obey. I'm careful to wind the hem of my shirt around the chain on my neck that still holds that ring right above my heart. When I'm confident it'll all come off in one piece—gracefully—I pull it over my head and drop it on the floor. It falls softly, no sound made. *What was I going to do in a hookup with anyone else? Probably the same thing, I guess.*

Katrina runs her fingertips down my chest and my abs, then hooks them at the top of my jeans and tugs me closer to her.

I let her. I raise my hands to cradle her face and savor the feeling of her soft skin underneath my calloused hands. I tip her head towards mine and brush my fingers into her hair, lifting it from her shoulders and draping it across her back. "Are you sure this is okay?" I whisper.

She nods.

My lips touch hers. She tastes like hibiscus and honey, and it's the beginning of my undoing. I knew I was lighting a matchstick, that she's pure gasoline. Any *seeing through* of this would have eventually led here. I just wonder what Nathan and Beatrix are going to have to say.

Katrina chases my thoughts away with the sound of my belt buckle coming undone. Her painted fingernails drag along my thighs as she pulls my pants and boxers down my legs.

She's on her knees.

Meaningless, I remind myself desperately.

Her eyes meet mine.

A chill rakes up my spine, and pleasure spins through my blood. Again: *This doesn't mean anything.* I try so hard to remove *all this* from anything we had in the past.

It doesn't work.

Chapter Ten

KATRINA

I WAKE THE MORNING AFTER with dread pooling in my stomach. The memories come back in fragments, in flashes. First, having my way with him on my knees. Then, the way he picked me up and threw me onto the bed. The hair pulling, the hickeys, the way the headboard creaked and slammed against the wall. *Holy hell, you probably woke everyone on this floor.*

I shift under the covers, finding the heavy duvet tucked up around my neck. The sheets are slick and dry on my legs; they smell like bleach and chlorine.

That's right. You went to the bar after, then to the pool. You waited 'til the bar closed then lounged by the water, waited 'til two in the morning and went skinny dipping for the rush. You were shit-faced. He carried you upstairs. You both went for round three.

I can still taste traces of my spiked lemonade and the slow-creeping headache that always follows the next morning.

I look to my left to find Corbin lying on his stomach, his mop of hair covering his face. His arms circle his head and his pillow. His face is so free of concern, so *easy* to look at.

My stomach twists, and with it, a deep ache in my belly. Dampness between my legs. Heat rises on my face. *What on earth have you done?*

Slowly, quietly, I locate my phone on the floor and grab it. I open my app menu and call a cab. There's no way I can be here when he wakes, otherwise one night will turn into another, and then I'll find myself right back in the predicament I was in before. *How can he want you when no one else did?*

But another voice says, *Isn't that what you want, though? For him to want you?*

I bite my lip to clear my head. Now isn't the time.

I slip out of bed and dress as quickly as I can without making a sound. I pick up my shoes and carry them with me. I take one last glance at Corbin, where he's still passed out in bed. He doesn't move, save for the slow rise and fall of his chest. Wincing at my own ridiculousness, I crack the door open and step out of the hotel room. It latches behind me.

In front of me, the sun is just peeking over the ocean. My breath catches. For a moment, I wonder what it would be like to go back into the hotel room and tuck myself back into bed next to Corbin's body, to let him wind his long arms around my body and press morning-breath kisses on my face and neck until we dissolved into more rebound sex. We'd throw the curtains open and gaze at this view until we had to check out. Then, we'd go down to the beach and talk about the last time we saw his parents and the way they looked at me.

That was then, I remind myself in horror. It would be so easy to fall back into that life.

So why don't you?

I look back at the hotel door.

Of course, I don't have a key.

So Uber it is.

Chapter Eleven

CORBIN

I WAKE TO A SLICE of sunlight burning into my eyes. When I sit up, I find that Katrina's side of the bed is empty, the covers deftly pushed back and crumpled. I sit up and rub my face aggressively.

I should have known.

I should have *expected*.

I did it then, and I'll do it again.

As I collect my discarded clothes off the ground, I wonder to myself, all the things anyone would wonder: *Why? Was I not good enough? Did she not enjoy our time together?* Last night as we swam naked in the pool, she whispered things to me with her wet, glistening lips, things I *swore* I would never hear her talk about again. She'd brought up the first time she ever met my parents and the horrible judgment they put on her shoulders.

Even after Katrina had long gone home, I listened to my father tell me all the ways Katrina was less than what I deserved. That I *deserved* someone of power and influence and esteem. But that was *his* thing, not mine. That was exactly why I loved Katrina so much: she had none of that. She let the world around her move her where it wanted. She lived in the wind, something that I've tried to mimic ever since I first met her.

The wind brought me here. Guess I may as well stay a while.

I pull my pants on and locate my wallet in my back pocket. The card Callie gave me is still tucked inside. I take it out and look at both sides. It's plain white with a royal blue stripe across the top and some finely printed information across the front.

ARCHER MOSLEY

REAL ESTATE AGENT

904-555-2109

I dial his number on my phone and listen to the line ring.

"Archer Mosley, how can I help you?"

"Hello," I say. My voice cracks so I clear my throat and start again. "My name is Corbin. I met your daughter Callie the other day, and she told me you can help me get set up in a long-term rental here."

"Can you tell me a little more about what you're looking for?"

"Three beds, at least two baths. My friends and I are in town, and we'd like to stay a while. Six months, ideally." I pick up my shirt and my necklace and Katrina's ring fall to the floor. I kneel to pick it up. The diamond ring sparkles resiliently in the low light of the drawn curtains.

"I've got just the thing you're looking for."

Chapter Twelve

CORBIN

"I STILL CAN'T BELIEVE HE found you a place on such short notice," Nathan says as he lugs his backpack through the front door. It's always surprised me how much he can pack in a simple carry-on during our road trips. "Damn, this place is nice."

The beach house sprawls out before us in an open floor plan. On each side of the door, there are two sliding doors.

We could open the whole living room up to the outside if we wanted to. The walls are painted a light, purple-toned gray, and a large white marble fireplace sits on the back wall of the living room.

"Who uses a fireplace in Florida?" Bea asks with a scrunched nose.

"Maybe in the winter," Nathan says. He shrugs. "I heard it snowed in '89."

A few modern-looking pieces of art hang on the tall walls, leading my eyes up to the vaulted ceiling.

"Thank God this place is furnished!" Bea's voice echoes down the hall. "I call the master bedroom!" A pause. "Whoo-wee, look at that *bed!* We'll be living like kings here!"

"Totally not fair," Nathan grumbles.

"Is too. It's like calling shotgun. You snooze, you lose, dude," Beatrix says.

I venture down the hallway after them. The wood floor underneath my boots is a welcome change from the murky green hotel carpet. I let Nathan pick the room he wants, then I settle for the last room left. Honestly, the gesture is more for them than it is for me. I might've footed the bill to stay here for the time being, but even now, I can't say how much of my time will be spent *in* the rental. Part of me anticipates trying to stay at Katrina's place, if she'll allow it.

The last room left is down the hall and around the right. The room has a vibrant purple accent wall and deep red sheets on the bed. They look nearly like satin; for the price I paid, I wouldn't be surprised. I wonder if Callie's father always finds the nicest places for friends of his daughter.

I place my backpack on a low-sitting paisley chair in the corner.

"I call dibs on the hall shower, Ben! Sorry, bro, but I gotta get this Florida *stank* off of me," Nathan calls from the hallway. The bathroom door slams shut.

I open the curtain to the evening sky and flop down on the bed. The room smells like wood stain and polish, and the sheets have an airy, flowery smell. I could fall asleep right away. My hand finds the ring on my chest, and my tired eyes close of their own accord.

I WAKE THE NEXT MORNING, fully dressed on the top of my bed. Distant clanking in the kitchen sounds, and slowly, the smell of eggs and bacon and tofu drifts down the hallway. I sit and put my elbows on my knees and exhale slowly. After everything that's happened, I feel as if I could continue to sleep for days on end. As long as it takes to forget the fresh memories of Katrina.

I ditch my clothes, pull the covers back, and crawl into the borrowed bed.

Sleep pulls me back under.

WHEN I WAKE A SECOND time, my room is blindingly bright. The sun douses my bed with warmth, and the sheets around my neck cook me in my own sweat. I throw them off and breathe deep. Drowsiness clings to me. I take a quick shower and throw a change of clothes on. On my phone, I make a reminder to buy myself some spare clothes for the rental, since I plan to stay a while.

I sit on the edge of my bed and stare into the depths of my phone. I open my contacts. Pull up Katrina's number. Stare for a minute.

"Hey, man, finally up?" Nathan knocks on my doorframe.

"Yeah," I say with a deep exhale. I close my phone and turn to face Nathan.

Nathan leans in the doorway, one leg crossed over another and hands in his pockets. He's wearing an all-black getup—his leather riding pants and a black tee with capped sleeves. His biker jacket hangs from his shoulders, three patches on the fabric. The first is a shield with four wings with a spiked halo in the center of the shield. Just below the first, there's a circle patch with two golden swords clashing. On the other side of his chest, a large compass is sown onto the leather. Our gang patches.

My father hated each one. That's exactly why Nathan sported them every chance he could—to hold a massive middle finger in my father's face.

"Wanna go out for lunch with Bea and me?"

I nod. At least it'll keep me from calling Katrina.

Everything feels dull in comparison to when I was with Katrina. Pulling on my shoes reminds me of waking up to her gone. Pulling on my jacket reminds me of how I had to check out of the hotel alone. Stepping out of the air-conditioned rental and into the Florida heat reminds me of the dreary drive back.

"Nathan and I got some tips from some locals on the beach this morning. You would not believe how friendly people are here. Sweet couple. We stood and talked for a while," Beatrix tells me. "Maybe tomorrow if you're not sleeping in you can join us for the sunrise. It's a cool bucket list item, anyway."

I nod numbly.

"They recommended a place called Timoti's Seafood Shak," Nathan says. "They've got vegan options."

I stand and follow him out into the living room. Sun drapes in through the open windows. We lock up behind us and swing onto our bikes. Or at least, Nathan and Bea do. It feels more like lifting lead over the back of my motorcycle, trying to swing my leg over.

The drive is a straight shot. Our rental sits on the North side of the island, tucked in a little grid-like span of streets. Once we get out to Atlantic Avenue, we take a right. Five minutes later we're crossing the light onto Centre Street, our main hub since arriving. We park our bikes on a side street with designated motorcycle parking. They look good together too. Although my motorcycle is a plain gloss-and-matte black, Nathan has painted yellow and orange hell flames across the wine-red body of his. Beatrix went for the finer details: her white bike has small spots of pale, storm blue in matte vinyl— on the brand name, on the tire rims, and one tasteful stripe across the sporty-sleek body. Her helmet hangs off the back, a Greek olive wreath stenciled out of the same vinyl.

Our bikes have been an ongoing joke. At the beginning of our friend group, there had been one more with us, and we called ourselves *The Four Horsemen*, designing our bikes accordingly. Beatrix chose *Conquest* as her bike's name, though Nathan argues her every time it comes up, insisting that it should be *Pestilence* instead, that a white and green design with biohazard warning labels would have been way cooler. And, fittingly, Nathan had claimed *War* for himself. My own bike represented *Famine*. The last member of our group, who had claimed *Death* for his bike, had dropped out, and ever since we've been on the search for a new fourth.

The Three Horsemen just doesn't have the same ring to it.

The idea for the gang had sat around in my head for years before it ever came to fruition; something about my father's religious lectures made me want to have fun with the idea. Instead, he called my friends and me *sacrilegious* and banned Nathan and Beatrix from ever setting foot in his home again.

It makes me wonder if anyone else sees our niche, religious jokes in the bike. I doubt it at first, as we walk away, then I remember—we are in the Bible Belt after all, and we drove past four different churches simply on our way here.

Nathan navigates us a street and a block over to a restaurant tucked under a wood and metal roof structure. There are at least a dozen picnic benches placed under the awning. Bea opens the door for us as we walk in.

The man at the register smiles big for us and takes our orders and lets us know we can wait outside.

I collapse on a bench right near the order window so I can keep the moving to a minimum. I feel like I've been sulking through molasses for the last few days after Katrina.

"So," Nathan starts, leaning in and sipping on his cup of water. "*You* didn't come back to the hotel the other night."

"Yeah, Ben, what was that about? You set up a terrible situation for *me*," Bea says jokingly, but Nathan punches her shoulder. "Nate tried to Netflix and chill me."

"Can't blame a guy for trying," Nathan says with a roll of his eyes.

When our food is called, I turn to grab it before they can ask me more questions. Apparently, they have longer attention spans than I give them credit for.

Beatrix looks at me through spiky black bangs. Her eyes twinkle at me mischievously, her sharp chin and high cheekbones angling her face into a feral grin. "You stayed with Katrina. Her place?"

"Hotel," I mutter.

"Get any action?" Nathan asks.

Beatrix elbows him.

I don't answer. Instead, I dig into the tacos on my tray. Flavor explodes in my mouth—all the right amount of Cajun seasoning, fresh lemon, ranch, and fresh tomato and lettuce.

"Well we both know what that means," Nathan says, wiggling his eyebrows. "Our boy got it more times than he wants to let on."

Beatrix rolls her eyes and lets out a sound of disgust.

I try my best not to think about Katrina through mouthfuls of my meal—of my lips on her neck, her collarbone, her breasts. My face turns red, and I shoot a death glare at Nathan.

Nathan just snickers.

"So what's the plan, Ben? Just hang around town until you figure out if she still wants you?" Beatrix asks. She digs into her salad box.

If they only knew she left before I woke, they wouldn't be saying the same thing... What I say instead is, "I don't have anywhere else to be. Plus, I like the town, and we have the rental for six months. A lot can happen in six months."

Beatrix raises her eyebrows but says nothing. "Guess I'll look for a job, then."

"I've got you for six months, if you need a spot," I tell her. I already covered our lunch. Or maybe I should say, my father did.

"Yeah, I know that, but who knows? There could be some fun job opportunities around town. If there's anywhere to find a fun job, it's gotta be here," Beatrix says. She tucks a stray strand of her short black hair behind her hair as she eats.

"Speak for yourself. I could use a vacation." Nathan shovels a spoon of tofu into his mouth. "As long as you're cool with it."

I nod. "Can't promise anything after the six months, though, after the lease is up."

"All good. I appreciate it," Nathan says.

A dark brown bird hops down onto our table and struts over to Nathan. He shoos it away, and the bird cocks its head and flutters to the ground to pick at crumbs between the cobblestone.

"Maybe I'll take up painting. Sounds like there are a lot of galleries around town." Nathan combs a hand through his white-blond hair, still munching on a mouthful. Every time he opens his mouth with food still inside, Beatrix fixes him with a dirty glare.

"Sounds stupid," she says.

"You're stupid," he says.

I roll my eyes and focus on my lunch. I would've thought that in their mid-twenties my friends would be above elementary comebacks, but clearly not.

"Anyway," Beatrix says. "I think you made a good choice. It's worth seeing things through with her. Girls love to be chased."

"Only if the guy's not a serial killer," Nathan says with food in his mouth, again.

Beatrix shoves Nathan's shoulder. "You're disgusting."

"No, *you're* disgusting."

"Dude, I bet you fifty bucks you can't get laid before me. Town limits," Bea says.

"You're fucking *on*, sister." Nathan grins manically at her.

"Word gets around in small towns," I warn them.

"Yeah, so everyone's about to know who's got the biggest dick around."

"You fucking wish," Beatrix says, stifling a laugh.

"*You* wouldn't know." Nathan flexes his arm, kisses his bicep, then puts a hand up to Beatrix as if to arm wrestle her.

Beatrix stares at me with a done-as-fuck expression, and a laugh slips through my own lips, catching me off guard.

"You're just trying to get your hand next to mine so you can size yourself up," Bea snaps. "Not happening."

"You're scared I'm stronger than you."

"I'll go," I say, wiping my hands on a napkin.

As soon as my elbow hits the table, Nathan pulls his arm away and lifts both his hands in surrender. "Nah, bro."

Beatrix and I dissolve into laughter, and Nathan takes his turn rolling his eyes.

"The couple this morning mentioned an event coming up. Maybe you could invite Katrina?" Beatrix finishes the fries beside her salad box then takes a few drinks of water. "I think they called it a…*Shrimp* Festival?"

"Whatever the fuck that means," Nathan adds in.

"Apparently it's the biggest event here locally. It happens next week. Plus, this would be a *great* time to let us meet her too."

"I saw you staring at your phone earlier," Nathan says. "You haven't spoken to her yet, have you?" A rare hint of sympathy sounds in his voice.

I shake my head.

"Call her," Beatrix urges.

My hand instinctively finds the outline of my phone in my right front pocket.

"Call her *now*."

I swallow the lump in my throat.

"Drinks on me tonight if he actually calls her," Nathan tells Bea.

Nathan never pays for drinks, so I pull my phone out and dial Katrina, just to see the surprise and dismay on his face. These are the little bets we play with one another. It feels good to have some semblance of family in this foreign town, in this foreign *situation*.

The line picks up but there's no voice on the other end.

"Katrina?" My voice cracks.

Nathan claps a hand over his mouth to keep from bursting out in laughter.

I flip him off. Aggressively.

"Ben," she says flatly.

"Hey, so, I just found out there's a festival coming up…and I wanted to know if you maybe wanted to go together."

Nathan's face turns red, and he scoots his tray out of his way, puts his head on the table, and his shoulders rattle out of control.

I flush with anger and embarrassment.

"Shrimp Fest?" I can hear the exasperation in her voice. "You're seriously still in town?"

"Of course I am," I say.

"How do you even know about Shrimp Fest?"

"The locals told us."

"No."

"What?"

"*No*, I'm not going to Shrimp Fest with you. What do you think this is, prom?"

Ouch.

"Alright, fine. I'll take someone else."

Bea's jaw drops across the table.

Adrenaline lights my nerves.

"Someone else?" Katrina scoffs. "*Who?*"

"Guess you'll have to come to find out," I tell her. I can nearly feel the heat fuming off of her from across the line. I hang up before she has the chance to say anything back.

Beatrix's eyes are popping out of her sockets.

Even Nathan is speechless for what seems like the first time in all of human history.

Chapter Thirteen

KATRINA

GUESS YOU'LL HAVE TO COME to find out. Corbin's words ring in my ear. The dead line is a static buzz.

I nearly throw my phone across the room.

How dare he?

He's trying to make you jealous, I reason with myself.

And you are. It worked. He made you jealous.

Grow the fuck up, I tell myself.

I put my phone on the bed beside me so I don't snap it in half. Deep breaths. *Deep breaths.*

The real question to ask yourself is, Why are you jealous?

I press my palms into my eyes.

You still want him.

Of course I still want him. How could I not? When he treated me like the only thing in the whole universe. When he touched me like I was worth more than gold. When he taunted and teased me in bed *and* like this. How could I not *still want him?*

Fine. If he wants to play dirty, I'll play dirty too.

ONLY ABOUT A MONTH AFTER I first moved to Amelia Island, I learned about Shrimp Fest. It was the biggest event of the summer, maybe even more so than the Fourth of July. Shrimp Fest was celebrated, according to the locals, to commemorate how the shrimping industry put Amelia Island on the map. But in reality, the festival isn't *wholly* based on shrimp, or at least, not from what I can tell. Sure, the locals say the main food truck food you can buy is mostly shrimp, but thanks to the island's history—it sounds like—Shrimp Fest is also an excuse to dress up like a pirate.

So I plan to dress up as the sluttiest, most irresistible pirate around.

Even with the time that's passed—even with Corbin's infrequent but delicately placed texts asking me if I've changed my mind—I'm still as blazing mad as I was when he first challenged me. I hadn't changed my mind; the only conclusion I've come to is to make sure that when he sees me at the festival, his jaw hits the ground.

I spend a few days finding pieces for my masterpiece. I decide on a pirate twist—I'll be a mermaid-turned-pirate.

It all came together when I found a cute shell-styled push-up bra while shopping for something sexy. It's not as if I *don't* expect Corbin and me to have another run-in without some sort of inner turmoil-turned-sexual-frustration. I only plan to make it much harder for him to move on, if that's his goal.

I stand before my bathroom mirror, tugging on each item I've pulled together to make sure everything is sitting as it should. Cleavage is sparkling—thanks to some incandescent body glitter. The waist is snatched, courtesy of a sea-green corset I found online. Hips are bedazzled with chains of pearls and beads. A long brown skirt hangs from underneath the corset; it's thick and layered at the top but dissolves into wispy, sand-brown sheer fabric near my boots. My wedges conveniently pass as modern pirate-style boots.

I've styled my hair into a mix of loose curls and thin strings of braids tied shut with more beads, along with a feather for good measure. My biggest, gaudiest gold hoops hang from my ears; and I've settled on an asymmetrical pearl necklace that spans across my neck and shoulders, alternating between a cluster of pearls and see-through thread that makes the pearls appear to be floating on my skin.

I turn in the mirror, twist my heel to jut my hip out from under the slit in my skirt. Can't forget the thigh strap. All along my leg, too, I brushed a teal blue eyeshadow over net stockings to leave a checkered, scale-like pattern up my leg.

He won't be able to resist himself.

I grin at my savage reflection. Even my makeup suits the look—a wicked sharp cat eye with two pearl beads glued symmetrically underneath each eye.

Before I call it finished, I spritz some perfume over myself and slide a coral-shade lipstick across my lips. My typical purse is replaced with a fanny pack that looks also very pirate-y, with a large brass ring and two different-sized pockets that lay flat on my hip. *Now* the look is complete.

I call an Uber to Centre Street, knowing the traffic even on-island will be a headache. The driver lets me off as close as he can—Atlantic and 10th Street—and I tip him before he drives off.

The sidewalks are flooded with people walking towards Centre Street. Everyone looks a little different. Some wear Hawaiian shirts and Bermuda shorts. Others wear white sundresses to stave off the evening heat. Kids are dressed in a variety of pirate costumes—ranging from Halloween costumes to patchwork, made-at-home costumes like my own. Even adults are dressed as pirates, in many versions, just like the kids. I see several Sharpie mustaches on old and young men alike.

For a moment, standing in the sweltering May heat, I regret swapping my boots out for sandals. But anything for the outfit, I guess.

I merge into the crowd and walk alongside the strangers. I know what my first stop will be. *The Palace Saloon.* Not only could I use some liquid courage, but I'm pretty sure that's exactly where I'll find Corbin and his mysterious date.

As I walk, a few girls compliment my outfit. Others just stare and judge. The only thing I'm worried about is if I'll make it through the night without my bra turning into water bags.

All down Centre Street, the streets are lined with fantastic vendors. Booths host huge displays of all kinds of art. Metal prints hanging in one booth have such high resolution that it makes you feel as if you're swimming right in the ocean you're looking at. Metal sculptures of crawdads and crabs and, of course, shrimp hang in another. Handmade jewelry is another popular pick, with multiple vendors showcasing their own unique styles—resin jewelry, spoon jewelry, estate jewelry. Part of me is blown away at the magnitude of the festival; I've *never* been to anything like this in Chicago. Maybe it's because I never looked.

Finally, I make it to the doors of the Palace Saloon. I'm IDed at the door and given a hot pink, paper bracelet to wear. "So the bartenders know you've been IDed," the bouncer says to me.

I nod and step inside.

Music blares overhead.

The bar is already full of people, even just at five in the afternoon.

I order myself a shot and a beer and close my tab. For now, I have a mission to accomplish. Maybe later I'll open another one.

I down the shot with a burn and a wince and chase it with a sip of beer. My eyes water a little, but I savor the spice of the rum as it lingers in my mouth. The beer pales in comparison.

The alcohol swims in the pit of my stomach, and I take my beer to the back of the bar. The game room is full of people, too, and I have to shimmy my way through sweaty bodies, men wearing oversized tee shirts, and girls who look like they're way too young to be at a bar. When I make it into a clearing, I see him. Right where I thought he would be.

Corbin leans against a pool table with an ongoing game between a blond man and a black-haired girl, and he's talking to a striking blond woman who looks straight out of a Lands' End magazine. I grit my teeth but smile anyway.

His eyes find me almost immediately, as if he could sense I'd just entered the room. His lips are on the edge of a plastic cup, mid-drink. He coughs and sputters in his drink when his eyes land on me.

It seems, too, I'm not the only one who went crazy with an outfit. Though *his* still rings true to his own clothing style.

Corbin's wearing a pirate getup too—clunky leather boots, tight leather pants, a white, front-lace shirt, and his leather jacket on top. A cheap eyepatch is pushed up into his hair, tousling it just enough to make me think of my fingers there instead.

His date turns and follows his gaze right to me. She has big, doe-eyes and curly blond hair. A prettier, taller version of me with less freckles and more legs. Though, curiously enough, she isn't touching him, and he isn't touching *her*, and when she sees me her face breaks into a smile brighter than sunshine.

"Oh, Ben, is this your girlfriend?" she asks.

My eyes throw daggers at Corbin.

He's recovered from his fluster, and he grins back at me, a devious shade in his eyes.

He tricked you. He played into your jealousy and tricked you into coming. Now everyone knows you're a fool for him.

"This is Katrina," he says, motioning towards me.

The two playing pool also turn to look at me, and I feel my skin burning with anger and embarrassment. I take a deep drink of my beer and walk to Corbin, ignoring the others. "Can we talk?" I ask him under my breath.

Corbin's lips twist crookedly at me. "Don't you want to meet my friends?"

I'm at a loss for words.

Corbin puts a hand on the blond woman's back. "This is Callie. She's a local who's been showing us the ropes. And these are Nathan and Beatrix, my friends from up north. They came down with me on my road trip. You saw them the first night."

The two at the pool table take their turns waving at me. The blond man—Nathan—smiles suspiciously as his light green eyes flick between Corbin and me.

Beatrix just grins and winks at me. "Hey hot stuff," she says slyly. Then she turns to Nathan and whispers, "It all makes sense now."

Nathan stifles a laugh.

I glare at Corbin. "Can we talk? Alone. *Please.*"

Chapter Fourteen

CORBIN

KATRINA LOOKS LIKE SHE COULD breathe fire, the way she's glaring at me. It almost makes me want to laugh, how angry she is. But if I dare laugh, that'll be the end of the night for me, and we all know it.

I put my hand on the small of Katrina's back and lead her out into the courtyard. Her skin is damp to the touch but pleasantly warm on my cool fingertips. Her wild hair tickles the skin of my forearm in the humid night. I take another drink of my whiskey and Coke and steel my nerves for the impending conversation. Condensation wets my fingers. Sweat wets the back of my neck.

With the festival ongoing, even the yard is full of people, so I guide Katrina to the quietest corner available.

When we're out of earshot of the others, she whips around. "Are you fucking *serious*, Ben?" she snaps. "You tricked me." She pushes my chest with one hand, just hard enough to slosh the liquor in my cup.

I take another sip to hide my smile behind my cup. *And it worked.*

"I only told you I was going with someone else, not that it was a *date*. That was your own speculation."

"It's a *girl*," she hisses.

"That girl's name is Callie."

"*Fuck* Callie."

This time, the laugh gets away with me. "Relax, Kat. It was fun seeing you jealous for a few minutes, but Callie didn't do anything to you."

Katrina looks back toward the game room.

I put my fingers on her chin and turn her head back to me. "You look good," I tell her, gazing deep into her eyes.

The fire douses, if only but a little. Her burning eyes return to a muted shade of gold, her beautiful light brown.

My eyes drip down her face—to her lips, then the glittered length of her neck, then to her collarbones and the pearls scattered across them. My eyes land right where she wants them to, leaving me licking my lips. I take another drink of my whiskey; the buzz is setting in.

"You dressed up," she says, deadpan. Her voice has returned to a flat tone. Still, I know I'm not in the clear.

"I knew *you* would."

Her jaw flexes. She's always been a sucker for costume parties, always gone above and beyond to seduce me with her scandalous renditions of whatever theme she's going for. It surprises me that she and Beatrix never met before tonight, that those two circles of my life

never overlapped. Beatrix is the same kind of extra; the two would get along great.

"Now we look like we came together," I tell her, looping my arm around the back of her neck and drawing her closer to me.

She cranes her neck to stare up at me. "Do you like her?"

"Who?"

"Callie, Ben. Do you like Callie?"

"Can you better explain the question? Do I like her as a person, or…?" I can't help it. I love seeing her eyes flare.

"Do you like her *romantically?*" Katrina bares her teeth as she says the words.

"Maybe if I'd never met you, I'd have room in my heart to consider her."

"Fucking liar," Katrina spits.

"Am *not.*" My lips are nearly on hers.

Katrina doesn't pull back. Her beer dangles in her hand by my leg. I want to pick her up and make her drop it, to sweep her off her feet and surprise her, startle her into a laugh. She's still not smiling.

I lean in a whisper in her ear. "Want to have sex in the bathroom?"

Her skin warms under my touch. "You're drunk."

"Barely." I lean in and press a kiss to her neck. She tastes like salt and flowers, bitter and earthy.

She shivers.

"I won this round," I say against her neck. My pulse vibrates through me.

"This isn't a *game*, Ben." She puts a weak hand on me, as if she might try to push me away. So like all the times she's ever done this, I still my movements and wait for her decision. "This is our *lives* we're talking about. All bets off. What if I didn't show up? What would you have done?"

I open my mouth to respond, but she keeps talking.

"Is this your idea of not being tied down in a 'marriage?' Flirting with a random girl over drinks if I decide to not show up?"

"Of course not," I tell her.

Katrina's eyes flick back and forth as she surveys my face.

"Why are you so worried I'd give you up for someone else?"

She flinches, her nose scrunching and twisting the spatter of freckles there.

"There's *no one* like you, Katrina. I *love* you," the words come out of my mouth before my brain registers them. I curse inwardly, then outwardly, then go all in. "I love you, Katrina. I never *stopped*."

Her lips crash into mine in a dizzying rush. My drink splashes onto my hand. Her beer bottle presses up against my face as she wraps her arms around me in a full-body launch. The kiss feels like heaven, like some long-awaited reward, as if all my turmoil in the past weeks has paid off to some degree.

I recall the nights leading up to today briefly, of Nathan and Beatrix warning me against going through with my threat of taking someone else to Shrimp Fest. Of calling Callie and meeting her for lunch. Of spilling my guts out before her, telling her who Katrina was, about the night she left, how I ran into her here by chance. Callie's face reflected each of my concerns. Her sympathy for my heartbreak, her shock over my proposal, and more than anything, the way her face fell when I showed her the ring still hanging around my neck. The first words out of Callie's mouth were, "Don't ignore when God sends you good things. This is a sign." A more religious way of mirroring exactly what Nathan and Bea have been saying.

When Katrina's lips pull away from mine, I'm left wanting *more*.

Because what if it is true? What if this was the universe's way of telling me, *This is a good thing?* How do I get her to see the same thing? How do I convince her that this is a *good* thing?

I go in for a second, more passionate kiss. Her lips part easily for me. My tongue traces her lips. She tastes bitter here too, like the pale beer in her hand. I grab the back of her head and keep her there, pressed to me. Much to my surprise, one of her hands laces around my back too and sneaks right under the hem of my shirt. *Fuck, I can't get her close enough.* I need her skin on my skin, her hands pinning my hands, her mouth on mine, all night long.

Her fingers trace my belt loop from the base of my spine around to my front.

Just before Nathan clears his throat loudly and awkwardly. "Holy hell, don't bust a nut right here in front of everyone guys," Nathan says.

I'm gonna kill him.

Katrina pushes me away for real this time, her face completely red.

Nathan grins at her. "He's got it bad for you, girly."

"Don't call me *girly*," she quips back.

"Why not?" Nathan circles Katrina like she's his prey, and it makes even *me* nervous. I call him out on being weird, but he doesn't stop. He's sizing her up. "You're *tiny*."

Beatrix laughs behind me.

I look over my shoulder to find Bea and Callie watching the scene unfold. Which means they watched our kiss unfold, too. *Damn it.* Guess I should've known better than getting privacy in the height of drama. Nathan and Bea are drama junkies; we've had one too many all-nighters watching trashy reality shows with hot singles dressed in strings barely passing as swimsuits. God knows they live on the stuff.

"I can see why Ben likes you. Fiery as all Hell broke loose. God, and *look* at you." Nathan looks blatantly at Katrina's chest.

I lurch forward, but Bea lunges to grab me. She detains me quickly with a twist of my wrist behind my back. Quiet and discreet, ever her superpower. No one would know I almost jumped Nathan right then and there.

"Do not punch him. You'll get us thrown out," she whispers angrily. Then, she snaps at Nathan. "Nate, quit egging them on. Katrina's off-limits for our bet. You can't even *try* with her."

Nathan winks at me, and I nearly pull out of Bea's grip.

"Okay fine." Nathan relents with his hands in the air. He walks past me and leans in. "You know I'm just kidding, right?" His voice is level, and I know he is, but it doesn't stop that terrible, possessive side of me from surfacing.

"Fuck off, man," I tell him.

Nathan shrugs it off and disappears back into the bar.

Katrina looks between us with her jaw hanging and confusion lining her brows. "Is he normally like that?" she asks, flabbergasted.

"More or less," Bea says.

Chapter Fifteen

KATRINA

I'M NOT SURE IF I want to laugh or cry. I stare at the group—and Nathan's disappearing back—and they study me in return. Beatrix is dressed like a slutty pirate too, something I would acknowledge verbally if it weren't for the blatant humiliation Nathan had shown me not one minute earlier. I look down at the fake green grass below my boots to ground myself. Close my eyes. Breathe deep. I can still taste the salt in the air, this far from the ocean.

Why did you come here? Why couldn't you just let it slide?

Exhale.

You know why. You just won't admit it to yourself.

"They're setting up for karaoke in twenty," Nathan shouts across the courtyard, a silver bucket of beer clattering in his hand. "Who's up first?"

I excuse myself, telling Corbin that I promise I'll come back, that I just need a moment, and he offers to hold my beer then lets me go. I can *feel* his eyes burning holes in my back as I walk down the sidewalk to a less populated stretch of the street.

"Hey!" Beatrix calls behind me. She jogs to catch up.

"I just need a moment," I tell her.

"It's okay. We don't have to talk." Beatrix matches my pace as I round the corner then make my way to Front Street. I find a spot near the grass and sit straight on my butt. My legs drain of strength a moment later, leaving me wondering how they were ever holding me up to begin with. They wobble with exhaustion, with emotion.

Beatrix sits beside me. Silently.

What a relief.

I collapse on my back and stare at the sky. The sun stares—brutally—back.

Beatrix does the same.

"People are going to look at you weird," I say.

"People are going to look at *you* weird. Fuck. I sound just like Nate. I'm sorry," Beatrix says. She laughs to herself. "Besides, I don't care."

I say nothing. The setting sun lessens in strength with every passing minute. My breaths regulate. My heart slows.

This is all too much.

"I was trying to get away," I tell Beatrix. Without context, it makes no sense, and I only realize this after the words have left my mouth. I'm not sure why I'm confiding in her. I turn my head to look at her, and she turns her head and stares back at me. An invitation.

She's giving me space, a safe place, to express my feelings.

"I guess I just got scared. Not just now, the first time."

"I wouldn't blame you if you said just now. Nate's scary as all fuck."

I chuckle lightly. "No, I mean, the proposal."

"That's understandable. I don't think I could ever, personally…" Beatrix's blue eyes shift like water, moving across my face. She looks for something there, and she finds it. The pools of her eyes glimmer sweetly, a change from the rough exterior I've seen her show in our last run-in. "But he's a good one, Ben. You wouldn't be making a mistake."

"It's not that…" The grass beneath me pricks my exposed midriff, and I scratch the spot it touches. The earthy scent of the ground is a welcome change to booze and *Ben*. Seagulls call overhead. And even still, where we sit, the hum of the bar music can be heard over the top of the old town buildings. "I've never felt *wanted*."

"Trust me when I tell you, he wants you more than he wants his own life."

"It's not that I don't believe you, that I don't believe him when he says that… It's just…" *No one ever wanted you before, so how could he really, truly want you now?* "Do you think he'll get tired of me, you know, if I did marry him?"

"Hell no." Beatrix laughs, and it sounds like silver wind chimes. "You are surprising enough to keep him on his toes for the rest of his life, I can promise you that much. You should have seen his face when you left."

"Ugh," I mutter, covering my face.

"You should do a song with me," Beatrix says. "Sing some karaoke with me. It'll loosen your nerves a little."

"I don't think I'm drunk enough for that."

Beatrix props herself on one arm in the grass. Her outfit—a low cut, white, ruffled blouse and her black biker jacket—hangs open on her flat chest. "I can get you drunk enough for that, if you want."

"It's no wonder you and Ben are friends," I moan. "I swear he's said those exact words to me before. Tonight."

Beatrix's eyes widen and she laughs brightly again. "Oh, *no!*"

"Oh, yes, unfortunately."

Beatrix sputters out a loud cackle. "For fuck's sake. He's so whipped for you. C'mon. Sing with me. It'll drive him crazy to see you on stage. We usually all go up and do it together. It'll be like you're officially *one of us*." Beatrix nudges my shoulder lightly.

"Okay, okay. After a few shots."

"You've got yourself a deal, girl." Beatrix grins wildly. She jumps off the ground and helps me up. "Super cute outfit, by the way. I love the detail on your leg." She gestures towards the crisscross, teal, net pattern on my skin.

"Thanks," I say, smiling down at my crafty makeup work. "I saw it online, and it looked easy enough."

We walk back to the Palace together, and I take a moment to appreciate the sun and the way it casts golden streaks of light across the streets. Vendor's white tents turn orange. Buildings are gilded with yellow windows. The smell of the paper mills on the island greets me with notes of cedar and pine. Yet, all this beauty doesn't stop my stomach from doing little nervous somersaults inside me upon Beatrix's proposition. Karaoke. Of course they would do karaoke.

Corbin has never been exactly *extroverted,* but I know better than anyone that his ego is big, and his humor is sly and sassy when it shows. It makes sense, for him to go out for karaoke nights with his friends.

We cross the street and walk back to the bar. On the newly poured pavement below me, I notice an etching that says "4HA." It rings a bell, somewhere deep inside me, but the memory isn't clear enough to make out. Someone must've made the mark recently, as this whole stretch of concrete is still white and clean.

Back at the bar, Beatrix and I regroup with the others. From the looks of it, Corbin and Nathan have made up and are chatting with new drinks in hand—beer for both of them. They're all standing under a stretched cover and golden-bulb patio lights that make them look both—regretfully, in Nathan's case—straight out of a magazine. As we approach, they turn and watch us. I take in their starkly different features—Nathan's ghostly, white-blond hair that sways like feathers in the low breeze. His light eyes track and analyze his surroundings with cool indifference. Corbin, on the other hand, gazes at me from behind spiky clumps of his dark brown hair, with eyes sultry enough to make me melt on the spot.

I can barely fathom him watching me with those eyes.

Beatrix slaps a hand down on my shoulder, tearing me out of my thoughts. "Y'all ready for some karaoke?"

Nathan lets out a holler and my nerves go electric "Hell yeah, bro!"

"First round of shots on me," Beatrix says. She leaves me with Corbin and Nathan and Callie. "C'mon!"

Nathan and Callie follow, and I'm left with Corbin and his eyes that see right through my brave face.

"You're gonna do karaoke with us?" he asks.

I nod.

The corners of his lips point downward in a look of amusement. "By the way, I told Nate if he ever hits on you again, I'll skin him alive."

All bark, no bite. Classic Corbin. Though based on what I've seen of their friendship, I find myself believing that Nathan would respect Corbin's wishes.

"Thank you," I tell him. "It means a lot."

"Does it?" Corbin challenges. He offers me his beer bottle, and I take a sip. It sizzles sourly on my tongue.

Corbin knows better than to ask. He knows how irritated I get when men are openly disrespectful like that; that I will take it upon myself to call them out at the cost of my own public image. So I do appreciate it; it does mean a lot. He put himself on the line instead of letting me do it. I guess, in his mind, maybe that is confirmation that I still care. About how I look with him. About *us*.

I nod again, finding that we've grown closer, like two magnets on water. His hand is close enough to brush mine. His breath, close enough to taste.

"If we don't go now, Bea and Nate will steal our shots, and you'll have to sing sober," he whispers.

I can smell the whiskey on his lips. I would wonder how he was still standing if I didn't know his drinking habits. It seems his tolerance has improved, if only but slightly.

Corbin's free hand snakes around my waist, and he guides me back through the bar. His friends are already waiting for us there, with a row of rainbow shot glasses filled and ready.

"Second round's on me, if y'all agree to sing a duet," Nathan says.

"Fine," Corbin says.

Nathan's eyes latch on me.

"Fine," I mumble.

Nathan nods at the bartender then grabs the green shot glass. Beatrix grabs blue. Callie grabs red. Corbin grabs purple. I snatch the yellow and orange.

"Cheers to second chances," Nathan says.

"Cheers," Beatrix and Callie chime in.

"Cheers," Ben purrs, looking me dead in the eyes.

"Cheers," I mouth the words back, not quite sure of where my voice went. I down the first shot, then the second to catch up with everyone else.

The bartender is pouring another set.

Nathan and Beatrix are laughing with Callie.

Callie isn't looking at Corbin at all.

And Corbin is only looking at me.

The tequila goes straight to my head, making my pulse quiver inside of me. *You should have had more than a salad for lunch.*

Chapter Sixteen

CORBIN

KATRINA TAKES THE DRINKS LIKE a champ. It doesn't come as a surprise, either. She's always been able to drink me under the table.

Nathan covers the tab for the second round, and I feel the chronic pain and stress slipping from my joints and back. The alcohol is starting to go down easier—which is never a good sign. I doubt I'll remember anything tomorrow.

We make our way back out to the yard. There is someone singing on stage—nailing a classic eighties hit with surprising accuracy. Nathan says something under his breath about forgetting karaoke was going on tonight because the singer was so good. We all agree that we thought she could be the performing band—besides Bea, who seems to always pay more attention than Nathan and I combined.

"Let's go first," Beatrix says to Nathan.

Nathan shrugs and follows Beatrix to the side of the small wooden stage. Once they're done whispering to the DJ, early 2000s music starts blaring out of the speakers. It's a bassy song with hand-clap sounds for a beat. I place it immediately as a song Nathan has sung before—usually when he hears it playing in stores or bars or clubs. Nathan starts singing, just as loudly and obnoxiously as the original recording. When Bea chimes in with her gravelly voice, she's stifling a laugh. I can hear it in her voice, the tone of joy and happiness she only has while she sings.

Their voices mold together perfectly—a blend of Nathan's nasally, confident pitch and Bea's choppy, lower pitch. They know it as well as anyone who hears them—their voices complement each other. Like brother and sister. They've always enjoyed singing karaoke together, and it shows. Nathan's face is light and carefree, and Beatrix is smiling more than I've seen in days.

A small crowd forms in front of the stage to watch and jive to the beat. A small group of young women dance in a circle by the corner of the stage, plastic cups in hand. One of them screams at the top of her lungs, *"I love you, blondie!"* and Nathan turns to her, mid-lyric. His eyebrows hit his forehead, a grin splitting his face. Then, he shoots Beatrix a sly smile. All at once I remember their ongoing immature bet—whoever gets laid first wins fifty. I roll my eyes, knowing as soon as Nathan gets off-stage, he'll beeline to the girl screaming at him from the ground. Much to my surprise, when they're finished, the whole group of girls swarms him. He beams like a child at Beatrix, who sticks her tongue out at him then struts past, right back to us.

"You're up, boss," Bea says. "And you, hot stuff."

I look at Katrina. She looks like she's about to barf.

"We don't have to…" I tell her.

Katrina drinks from a beer bottle—I'm not sure where she got it—and steels her eyes and posture. "I'm ready," Katrina says.

"What song?" I ask her as we walk to the stage together.

"Breaking Inside by Shinedown," she tells me.

Of course. Our song. From our first week of dating. She'd sent it to me and texted, "His voice reminds me of yours." The song itself wasn't inherently romantic. It was more of a plea for help; I'd related to it back then, between my father's estrangement of me and generally feeling out of place in my circle of rich friends. They'd never felt like friends. In the pit of my stomach, I wonder if Katrina is trying to tell me something with the selection.

Katrina white-knuckles the railing as she climbs onto the stage. The DJ passes her a microphone, and she puffs out a small breath. Bracing herself for what's to come. I've seen her do it before, specifically before meeting my parents.

The DJ passes me a mic next.

The small TV screen on the stage lights up with white lyrics on a black background.

A small wave of nausea swims in my stomach with the collected assortment of liquor in there. I take a deep breath, focus on the electric guitar chords I know so well. Lyrics roll from my mouth easily; I've sung this song at karaoke before, drunk out of my mind. It's second nature. When the song reaches the chorus, Katrina harmonizes with my singing, quietly, shakily. Her eyes are on the crowd, wide with adrenaline. I walk to her as the second verse approaches notoriously sung by Lzzy Hale.

I bet you sing like her, I remember saying to Katrina the first time I heard the song.

You'll never know, was her response.

I wonder if she's thinking about that right now too. Katrina's lips part slightly.

Beats turn into eternities. My heart hangs by a string, suspended in the silence between the instruments.

The first words resound from her chest.

My heart twists mercilessly at the melody of her lyrics, of her voice, of *her*. It's breathtaking, like the song of a siren at sea—low, compelling, smooth as the ocean at dawn.

I can't take my eyes off her, her coral-colored lips, the way they curve around the story she sings, the way her chest heaves for breaths.

I would go anywhere for her in that moment—cross the world and the seven seas. Wherever she is, I would be too.

When it's my turn to sing again with her in the chorus, I'm at a loss for words—staring star-struck at the way the bright stage lights make her skin look as if she's glowing like the sun. Her stray curls and split ends form a hazy halo around her round face.

My heart is hers, forever.

She gazes at me as she sings the second chorus alone, as if she knows I'm completely and utterly hers, from this moment on.

At the bridge, I find my voice again. I sing with her as if it's my last time to profess my love. Lyrics rip from my lungs, pleading, begging, baring my soul to her. As if this is our moment of all or nothing. I could listen to her sing for the rest of my life and never tire of it. I sing as if I'm begging her to never stop, to never leave my life again.

Her eyes are liquid fire.

The end of the song has us panting for breath.

We're close again—we've gravitated towards each other, orbited each other until we're right here—a breath away—*again*.

I pull Katrina to me, and her body hits my chest with a sharp exhale. I lean in and kiss her with everything I've got. Drinking in the taste of her mouth—of stale beer and tequila, of the tension in her. She unwinds in my arms, but adrenaline is still coursing through my veins.

Chapter Seventeen

KATRINA

Everything else is an afterthought. The sound of the crowd, the sweat on my back, the nervousness pooling in my stomach. Corbin and I tumble down the hall, all arms and hands and gropes and gasps. His fingertips dig into my ass, crumpling my skirt and hiking it up. His breath is in my ear, on my neck, sending shivers across my skin.

We stumble into the women's bathroom. I grab at his collar, crashing into another kiss, and pull him into the stall on the far left that's its own room with a full door. He swings the door shut and locks it, taking a good look at it as he does so. The thought seems to flow between us: *If we're quiet, no one will know we're in here together.*

As if I would care much anyway…

Corbin takes me by the hips and positions me in front of the sink, and I lean forward slightly, bracing my hands on the porcelain edge. I can hear his belt buckle jangle, his pants unzip, and the rip of a condom package.

I glance up at the mirror to find Corbin's eyes fixed on me, lips parted ever so slightly. Heat pools in my stomach, dripping lower and lower.

Everything is a blur, a rush, of pleasure and adrenaline. The sound of *us* fills the stall; our bodies, our breathing. My skin feels as if it's covered with millions of glowing bioluminescence, glittering in the aftermath of the tequila and the taste of him. The alcohol is still blurring my mind just enough that I'm not thinking about what happens after this, just what happens *now*.

We fall over the edge together.

Corbin places kisses on my back, down my spine. A low rumble sounds in his chest. "Fuck," his word comes out as an exhale. "You're perfect, Katrina." A whisper.

I want him *more*. I want to go again, against the wall.

I turn, and my dress falls over the back of my thighs; my skin is hypersensitive and aware of each brush of fabric. I feel cold from the lack of him.

Corbin's eyes are electric on me, his face flushed, his hands shaking as he pulls his condom off. He looks down, his hair falling in front of his face.

My stomach tightens at the sight. He's so attractive, so magnetic. I step closer.

Corbin peeks up at me shyly. His eyes are dilated from intoxication.

I lean in for a kiss.

His breath tickles my lips. He closes the distance. His hand cups the back of my head. He drinks me in.

My legs go weak, as if they weren't already. I want to beg him to take me again, but a stall door slamming outside of ours rattles us both. The shock sends another stream of adrenaline into my blood.

"How do we get out of here?" Corbin whispers conspiratorially, a flicker of a smile on his face.

I stifle a laugh. Then I *really* laugh at the craziness of our drunken stupor. He laughs too and his voice echoes, deeper and further than mine. I hush him quickly.

"You go out first. Tell me if it's clear."

Corbin tosses his condom in the trash, and we wait for a moment, listening.

We hear the toilet flush right outside, the metallic bang of the stall door, then the bathroom door creaking shut. I peek my head out and look around the bathroom. All the stalls are empty and stand open. "You're clear if you move fast," I tell Corbin. I usher him out from behind me. "Go."

"What about you?" he asks.

"Hygiene first," I whisper sharply. "*Go.*"

Corbin doesn't linger; he must be as worried as I'm becoming about getting caught. I can't imagine being allowed anywhere near the bar after our sexcapade. Once I watch Corbin safely exit the bathroom and the door swing shut after him, I take a moment in the stall I'm in. I breathe deep. My stomach is still fluttering from the excitement of it all. I glance at my reflection in the mirror. My cheeks and collarbones are splotched red with passion. It makes me think of all the times before, all of the many midnight romps that led to me looking just this flustered, this warm, this *girlish*. It sounds silly, but the sex flush makes me feel and look *pretty,* and I have never been one to openly call myself that. I was able to recognize my own attractiveness, but this look—this softness in my face and my eyes—I only ever see after *him*.

I take a moment to pee—to save myself a week of a hassle—and then I steel my nerves for a second time tonight. I leave the bathroom, feeling more embarrassed than ever. Eyes down. *Praying* Nathan isn't right around the corner. I know it now—I would never hear the end of that if he was just standing there waiting for blackmail to hold over Corbin.

Before rejoining the others, I go to the bar and order another shot of liquid courage. It goes down fast and easy, and regretfully, makes me consider taking Corbin home. I could leave now. I could avoid the attachment. I wouldn't even have to wake up in a sun-warmed bed with his sleep-tousled hair on the pillow next to mine. I wouldn't have to try to resist the warmth of his skin or sneak out of the situation or call a cab. After all, it's only a one-night stand if it's *one night*. Two is dangerous territory. *Third time, you're a goner.*

I order another shot.

The bartender eyes me warily but serves me anyway.

I must not look *that* drunk. Either that, or I look like I need it.

My thoughts pull me back under the surface of my mind, down into a riptide of emotions. If I take Corbin home, it's nothing like a hotel. There is no easy out. But I want to take him home. Part of me *wants* to feel the angst of some complicated, tangled situationship and the rush of lust and love that comes with it. It's been too long since I've felt anything. And sure, true one-night stands could scratch the itch, but they're nothing like *that*. Nothing like *him*. Corbin fills some hollow corner of my heart with meaning and purpose; one-night stands often leave me reminded of that horrid truth. That no one really wants me.

No one but him, my mind whispers back to me.

That's the truth, and I know it. No one wants me but him, and I can't figure out why exactly it is that he even wants me.

Find out, that stupid voice urges.

I swear at my own inner monologue.

You could leave right now, a second inner voice.

Thank God therapists can't read minds yet. Regardless, maybe that's the exact reason I've stayed out of therapy all these years.

The music gets louder around me with the next song that plays. Someone beside me at the bar shoulders me then apologizes profusely and offers to buy me a drink. Fleetingly, I wonder if the shove was a clever way into the conversation, but the bartender refuses me the drink. Not that I asked. Things are beginning to swim, I realize.

You should find the others.

But what are you going to do?

Are you going to take Corbin home?

Are you going to let him drive home on the back of his bike?

Neither of you should be driving.

Call a cab.

SHUT UP!

A hand clamps on my shoulder, and I swing around to face Beatrix. She looks at me with concern on her face, a wrinkle between her black eyebrows, above her crystal blue eyes. *Are you okay?* She mouths the words.

I can't hear her over the music. I nod.

Beatrix leans in. "We're going to call it a night. Do you want me to drive you home?"

Either she's being nice or she's trying to hit on you.

A pause. "I don't want you to feel like you have to go home with Corbin, if you don't want to."

"I want to," I slur.

Beatrix's eyes widen at me. "Are you sure?"

I nod again. My eyes are getting heavy.

"Okay. I just wanted you to know that I'm here for you, if you need a girlfriend in your corner. I might be Corbin's friend, but I'm not about to let him take advantage of you when you're shitfaced, girl."

I nod and hug Beatrix in a silent *thank you.*

Her hands tentatively touch my back. "C'mon, let's get you to Corbin."

Chapter Eighteen

CORBIN

SUN TURNS MY EYELIDS PINK. I wake slowly. Nausea is the first thing I feel. Stiffness in my muscles is the next. When I turn my head, a headache pounds against my skull like a sledgehammer.

Fuck.

It takes a moment to recall the night before, but when I do, I let it replay through my memories on a slow, gratuitous loop. I should be ashamed of myself, but I'm not. Not for asking Callie to get in on my revenge stint on Katrina. Not for fucking Katrina in the bathroom. Not for allowing her to throw herself at me at the end of the night. Of course I would take her home, even if she left every morning. She should know by now that I would go to the ends of the earth for her, that I would fair any conditions she placed on me, on us, on our relationship—or whatever this is.

I drove her home on the back of my motorcycle. I was barely sober enough, and the dark morphed around us as we drove. She guided me to her little cottage on Tarpon Avenue. The house was tiny, a little white square with a tall privacy fence that shielded her porch only. There wasn't much of a yard to speak of, only palm trees and gigantic succulents around the gravel and sand surroundings of her home. I'd wondered if she bought it or rented it, but before I could get my bearings to ask, she'd already poured us both a glass of black spiced rum and put one straight in my hand.

That's when I let go. I let myself get way too drunk. We had two more rounds of mind-numbing sex—once on the kitchen counter, then again in her bed. When we finally collapsed, her eyes rolled back and closed, and she didn't open them again. I watched her drift off to sleep, watch the tiny trickle of drool at the side of her mouth. I wondered if she would even remember any of this, if maybe instead she would wake and be horrified to find me right there in her bed with her. I would leave if she asked me to.

For a moment, even now, I consider rolling out of her bed and sneaking out before she wakes. She did it to me, after all. *Maybe it's time to give her a taste of her own medicine,* I laugh internally. But no. I'll stay.

I turn in her bed. It's stiffer than I care for, but her covers are mounting on us, like puffy clouds in the sky. I can't even see over the top. I squish an armful of cover down—realizing the duvet is made of down feathers—to find where she's lying beside me.

Her face is expressionless, just like I left it last night. Now, little rings darken underneath her eyes. Her cheeks are pale, no longer blushing. The rush of the alcohol has long faded, and I suspect, that just like me, when she wakes, she'll be morbidly hungover too.

I exhale slowly.

I could fall back asleep. I consider it. Hard.

I shuffle over to Katrina and run a hand over her warm arm. The heat radiating from her body pulls me in, and I'm done for. I close my arms around her, tilt my head towards her so that I can breathe in the scent of her wild, curly hair, and close my eyes.

A WHILE LATER, KATRINA SHIFTS beside me, waking me once again. She moans as she wakes—and not in a good way. Her moan *screams* pain, regrets, and hangover. It's a sound I've heard plenty of times over the course of our relationship. Before.

And just like before, I plant a handful of kisses on her face as she rouses.

"*No,*" she murmurs. Such a sweet sound, her tired voice. When her eyes finally open in a morning squint, she peers at me with confusion. Golden light touches her lightly, like gold-dusted fingerprints across the freckles on her face. "Ben?" she whispers.

Just as I had guessed.

"We went to the palace last night," I remind her.

It dawns on her face as the seconds pass in comfortable silence.

She nods.

"You wanted me to come home with you."

A pause. Then tentatively, "…I remember."

"I can go, if you'd like," I offer.

She shakes her head, making a ruffling sound on the pillows beneath us. It carries. "No. Stay. As long as you make me breakfast, you can stay."

I chuckle and wrap her up in my arms again. She buries her face into my chest, her hands lacing around my back. *I could stay here forever,* I think to myself.

Katrina breathes gently on my chest, her fingers flexing and relaxing like a cat's paw on my side. It's been so long since we've been together like this, quiet in the morning. There's something different about morning cuddles; they always seem so much more raw, more authentic, as if it's just her soul lying beside me, before the judgment of the world has tarnished her. Before other people have altered her into what *they* perceive of her. She is just *Katrina* here and now. No expectations. No worries. No distractions.

I thread my fingers through her hair. They catch on the tangles and knots in her unruly curls.

She leans closer to my touch.

"So what does this mean?" I ask her. I want to know more than anything. It's not like she thought she wouldn't have to answer this question. She knew the moment she took me to her place things would change for better or for worse. Just like it did last time, in Chicago.

WE MEET AGAIN AT THE same bar, over the same drinks. The glossy surface clicks underneath Katrina's fingernails. They're a deep mahogany color—but more brown than red. An interesting choice. I've just ordered her regular, and she nods at the bartender to allow me to foot her bill. Not as if I haven't tried the past few weeks I've courted her here.

"How do you know I don't want rum on ice?" she asks with a sly smile on her face. Playing hard to get.

"That was my second guess," I lie. Anything to look cool in front of her.

The bar is glassy and smooth all around us, painted in deep malachite chromes and onyx floors. Everything is at least partially reflective, giving the illusion that there might be eyes peering from every corner.

In hindsight, I realize just how different it felt there than it does here. In these memories, everything is picture-perfect, chic, classy.

Katrina is a different person here too, in this memory. Her curls are tamed more often than not—smoothed back into a high ponytail. Her dresses are skintight and lethal—always black, always red, never anything less dangerous. Dainty sleeves, sharp as a knife. Stilettos that could pierce my hand. I like this look as much as I like her now.

"What do you want from me?" Katrina asks as she sips her drink with dark red lips.

I try to keep from wondering what those lips would look like doing other things. "Company."

"A one-night stand," she says.

"To get to know you," I correct her. "You're different than my friends. I want to know why."

Katrina laughs, loud and bright and abrasive. Her eyes scour me— taking in my designer watch, my button-down shirt and loose purple tie, my slacks, my dress shoes. Her eyes seem to see the price tag on each item. "How so?" she asks.

Like she doesn't already know. "They're shallow," I tell her.

"Because they're rich," she guesses.

I nod.

"Because you're *rich. Is it your money? Or a trust fund?"* she says the words like they're poison, like she has something personal against them. It's the first time a girl hasn't thrown herself at me at the prospect of money. It only makes me want her more.

"My father owns a pharmaceutical company."

"So your kid's kids are set for life." Katrina takes another drink and rolls her eyes.

If she only knew I'd steal that line for years to come and only think of her when I said it. That I'd only think of our kids and what they might look like.

Katrina shakes her head. *"Fine. I'll entertain this conversation. Do you want kids?"* Her eyes pin on me then hold me still. I'm trapped by her gaze of fire and gold.

I almost tell her I'd have her babies but think better of it, knowing she'd kick me in the nuts and walk straight out of my life forever. *"Maybe,"* I tell her, *"with the right person."*

"Is the right person rich?"

"Does it matter, given my pockets?"

Katrina scoffs.

"Do you want kids?" I ask her.

"I don't know." Her eyes stay low, showing the glitter makeup on her lids that shimmers like fool's gold in the dim lighting of the bar. *"I want to commit my all to a child. It has to be under the right circumstances."*

I raise my eyebrows. That's a surprisingly deep confession for a bar conversation, *I think to myself. "And those conditions are?"*

"A stable home. A loving father for the child. My undivided time."

"What if I wanted some of your time, too?"

Her eyes flick up, fixing me with a fiery look. It's not exactly heated, but charged. Like she can see right through me, like she knows what I'm doing. Like she thinks she might let me actually try.

"Could you share me with a child?" she asks.

"Only if you could do the same with me."

At this, her eyes turn to smoldering embers.

I burn under her gaze. Her jealous gaze.

"You would be mine, first."

"That goes two ways, Freckles."

Her gaze turns icy hot. "It's too early for pet names, Ace."

I grin at her.

Reluctantly, mischievously, she grins back.

THAT WAS OUR FIRST NIGHT together. When she stayed a second night, I knew she was willing to see through whatever potential we had. But the success was short-lived and followed by a hot pursuit. A push and pull. One week it was *yes*. The next week it was *no*. I never did find out why—if it was me or if it was her. Finally, I just lent it to her personality. She's as fickle as the wind, and I'm the storm chasing her.

How much can really change? I wonder as I run my fingers through her hair. *Is she really going to let me in this time?*

I hold her a while longer, drift in and out of sleep lazily, before finally, I decide to get up and make Katrina some breakfast. I press a kiss to her temple then slip out of bed. I can't find my clothes anywhere on her bedroom floor, so I search the rest of the house. With my head pounding, I collect my shirt and conspicuously hidden necklace at the front door, my underwear and pants in the entryway to the kitchen. I've effectively lost my socks.

I've almost thrown up by the time I've picked all my clothes off the floor, dressed, then made my way into the kitchen to pour myself a glass of water.

I take a few moments to look around the kitchen, locating everything I need—first to cure my hangover headache, then to make Katrina a plate of breakfast. I find her food is limited to shelf-stable cans and cereal in the pantry and a few things in the fridge: almond milk, avocados, dairy-free yogurt, and a vegan butter alternative. I sigh as it all comes back to me. Her vegan diet was always the part of her that was high maintenance. Though, I have her to thank for the experience it added to my cooking. Now I know how to make *anything* taste good—thanks to the vegan tendency to rely almost solely on seasonings and spices.

By some miracle, I also find a bread maker on her counter and a small four-by-six-inch note of ingredients taped to the front. I search her pantry and produce—by another great miracle—all the ingredients to make a loaf of bread. I throw it all in and hit the start button. On the counter, there are some bananas. Toast and a banana just doesn't have the same ring to it as pancakes and blueberries, though.

Fuck, Kat, why do you have to make it so hard for me to do something nice for you?

I lean against the counter, defeated, and pull out my phone. I open up my food delivery app and search for *local bakeries*. A few pop up. I browse the options before finding one place with vegan-friendly options. My miracles must be running out quickly. I order a half-dozen donuts and two small coffees that cost more than my last tank of gas then put my phone on the counter and slump into her kitchen chair.

I hold my head in my hands, drifting again between sleep and memories.

Chapter Nineteen

KATRINA

THE SCENT OF WARM, FRESH bread floats through the house. I roll onto my back. My bed has *never* felt better. I feel as if I'm floating in the sky, weightless, in air the perfect temperature, not a care in the world.

Thankfully, I've slept off the worst of my hangover.

A gentle knock sounds on my doorframe.

I look up.

Corbin stands there in last night's pirate getup holding a small green and white box in one hand and a cup carrier with two steaming cups of coffee in the other.

"How did you knock?" I wonder aloud.

"The donuts don't spill out of the box," Corbin says with a charming smile. He raps the door frame with his knuckle again—box in hand—to show me. "Good morning, Freckles."

"Don't call me that," I snap. Unwarranted, an emotion pulls on my tongue and, "*Ace*," slips out in a cheeky reply.

Corbin only grins more, brown eyes twinkling in the daylight. "Hungry?"

I nod and push myself up into a sitting position.

He brings the coffee and donuts over to me and places the box on the bed next to me and the coffee on the bedside table. I immediately recognize the bakery as one that offers vegan and gluten-free options, and gratitude swells inside me. Corbin watches me tear into the box and stuff my mouth with the first donut I lay eyes on. It's a dense, cakey donut with blueberry and lemon icing. I close my eyes, taste buds watering, as I pause mid-chew to savor the taste.

"Thank you," I mutter, mouth full.

"You're welcome." Corbin plants a kiss on my forehead.

I gulp down the food, then take a sip of scalding coffee to chase it. It burns all the way down. I regret it so much, but at the same time, I've never really learned patience with hot coffee. Something about the bitter after the sweet gets me.

"Kat," Corbin says quietly.

I shake my head. "No. Don't start. Just..."

Stay. Tell him to stay.

"What is this?" he asks, a hitch in his voice. Like some small broken shard of our past life is lodged in his throat. "What are we doing?"

I look down at the remaining five donuts. They're all different, and I hate that I scarfed the only blueberry and lemon one down without savoring it more.

Finally, I find some arrangement of words after contemplating the donuts for a minute longer. "I—I panicked. I… I didn't realize you were *that* serious. I got scared," I admit.

Corbin sits silently.

"I'm sorry. I know I hurt you."

"You broke me in two, Katrina," Corbin whispers.

I swallow a lump in my throat and take another burning sip of coffee to distract myself from the pain in my heart. My chest hurts instead. "Can I try to put you back together?" I ask, stupidly. I look up at him through the steam of my coffee, hoping *somehow*, I manage to look irresistible—enough with my morning hair and likely puffy eyes—that he can't say no.

Corbin takes a deep breath in, his muscled chest rising and holding the breath. "I guess, Katrina," he says. He exhales. "But only if you mean it."

The lump in my throat is back. I nod weakly. "We have a bet, don't we?"

My mind goes back there, to that beach, to that bet. If he can convince me that I can stay just as wild as I am now, he can ask me to marry him. The irony.

DAYS TURN INTO A WEEK. A week turns into a month. The heat of early June seeps in through the windows and the broken window seals. Corbin and I have settled into a tentative way of life. He stays when he wants to be close, when I need him close, and the moment I need space, he offers it. He goes out with Nathan and Beatrix. He goes out on a motorcycle ride. He gets out of the house in one way or another, just enough that it leaves me wanting him more.

Every now and then, I go out with Corbin and Nathan and Beatrix. They asked me to join their bike squad; Beatrix even offered to help me shop for a leather getup—then she leaned in and whispered that she could help me find some *other* leather getups too if I needed. I couldn't help but laugh, which resulted in a snort, which resulted in a judgmental glare from Corbin and wiggling eyebrows from Nathan.

Moments like these make me almost give in. It's as if I've almost started to learn and really *understand* that Corbin and his friends are just as wild as I am. Even though I initially declined their invitation to join their gang, that didn't stop them from dubbing me *The Angel of Death*. Nathan claimed that since the Angel of Death really isn't one of the Four Horsemen—and rather just an edgy side character in the apocalypse—all I had to do was ride on the back of Corbin's motorcycle. I let them entertain themselves with the idea, knowing more often than not, that would be my method of traveling with him anyway.

Two weeks into their stay, they presented me with my very own helmet: a shiny, rose-gold thing that had hints of reddish flames. The visor was solid black, impossible to see into but not impossible to see *out* of.

Every morning is a sunrise motorcycle ride.

Every afternoon is lunch break with the gang.

Every night is his arms wrapped around me and the taste of his lips.

And he's right, it is wild. It's free.

I don't feel as scared as I thought I would.

This morning, I opted to stay home rather than go out with Corbin. He shrugged it off and left, not bothering to pressure me or try to sweet-talk me into spending time with him. It was a little surprising, as even though he's been wary with the affection, he *does* still try to sweet-talk me from time to time. Especially when it comes to riding around on the back of his bike. As if he wants everyone in town to know I belong to him. It's a fine line to walk, for both of us.

Lunch passes without a word from Corbin, and I expect he's met up with Nathan and Beatrix somewhere on the island. It isn't until evening rolls around that something doesn't quite sit with me about his absence. I think again about his dismissal earlier, the way he hadn't kissed me this time before he left. A pit opens up in my stomach.

He's giving you a taste of your own medicine. He's making you nervous on purpose.

Call him.

Don't call him. That's exactly what he wants.

I sit down on the dining room chair and hold my head in one hand and my phone in another. There are no text updates from Corbin save for the last—two nights prior when he invited me to join him and the gang at the Palace after I got off work. My stomach somersaults inside me.

I type, 'Hey, where are you?' then backspace it all. Then I try, 'Did I do something wrong?' then delete that too.

He wants you to squirm.

'Fuck you, Ace.'

Delete.

'Please come home.'

Delete.

'Where are you?' Again.

Delete.

Finally, I dial his number, words brewing in my mouth, ready to spit at any given moment that he picks up. Accusatory curses. *How dare you? Why are you playing games when we just got serious? Is this not serious to you?*

The line goes to voicemail. "Leave a message," Corbin's voice says in a deadpanned, muted tone. The line beeps.

I hang up and look at my phone.

I call again.

Voicemail. Again.

"Fucking, stupid…" I mutter to myself. This was probably all a ruse for him—get me to come crawling back then leave me high and dry to get back at me for what I did to him. I deserve it.

I try my best to get Corbin out of my head for the next hour, but it doesn't work. Every corner of my house now has something of his. In my bedroom—his small stash of condoms. In the kitchen—his coupons for his delivery app. In the living room—missing socks that have been swept beneath the couch. In the bathroom—his two-dollar toothbrush from the gas station.

This was all in his plan, and I know it. It makes my blood boil.

But when the sun starts to set, something else sets in: *fear.* What if he didn't leave? What if he just wasn't able to make it back for some reason? Which brings the next, terrible thought: *What if he got in an accident?*

I grab my phone and dial Corbin again. No answer.

I search my phone pointlessly, hoping for some way to contact either Nathan or Beatrix, but I haven't saved either of their numbers. However, I do know what rental they're staying in. I grab my keys and swing out the front door. As I walk to my car, another emotion punches me in the gut. My car. It sits in the glow of the sunset—rose gold, just like the helmet Corbin and his friends gifted me, a rare color on the road. The sleek SUV was a gift from Corbin, back when we were together in Chicago. He gave it to me, brand new off the lot, paid in full in cash. I'd felt like a princess when he first presented it to me. He knew he didn't have to express his love with money, that I would've much rather the love languages like touch and quality time, but I didn't refuse the gift; the car I'd driven before was an old, champagne-colored junker car on its last leg.

Stomach twisting inside me, I jump in my car and drive to Corbin's rental.

Chapter Twenty

KATRINA

BEATRIX OPENS THE FRONT DOOR to their rental, her face ashen and wide-eyed. She must already be thinking exactly what I'm here to say.

"Have you heard from Corbin?" I blurt out.

Beatrix shakes her head. Her choppy black hair swings around her face frantically. The low light of the porch shines an eerie light on her face, illuminating dark rings under her usually bright eyes. She's wrapped in a glossy black robe that's barely held together by a loosely tied belt, and beneath a sports bra and boy short underwear peek through. Gilded in black and gold in the sinking evening light, she steps aside and offers me entrance to the rental.

Inside is less of a mess than I expected, making my nerves uneasy. These two were as scary-sexy indoors as they were outdoors. As if to further my point, Nathan is lounging across the black leather couch wearing a pair of sweats and a crop top that shows off a surprising set of abs. It makes my stomach do nauseating flips inside me.

Nathan catches me looking and gives a nonchalant wink. "Howdy, Kat," he says in a very northern accent.

Beatrix reprimands Nathan immediately. "She hasn't heard from Ben either, Nate."

Nathan's face drains at that, as if he was under the impression that Corbin had been safely with me. Now, with me here—looking likely as deranged as a midnight grocery shopper in coffee-stained pajamas—he probably is putting the pieces together. Nathan stares at Beatrix. "We should call the hospitals."

"The hospitals?" I ask, but it comes out as more of a squeak.

"I'm actually listed as an emergency contact on his phone." Nathan stands, grabs his keys and pockets them. "That's if his phone *is* still in working order."

"That's counting on the EMTs seeing and recovering his phone at all, if it is."

My head spins violently. I sit on the footrest and hold my head. It doesn't help steady me. I just spin faster.

"I'll call the hospital," Beatrix says and then leaves the room.

Nathan walks up to me. Something about the way he moves—his wispy white-blond hair, his pale green eyes, his serpentine fluidity when he walks—sets me even more on edge. "You didn't break his heart again, did you?" Nathan asks in a whisper.

My heart jerks in my chest. I open my mouth once, but words fail me. "Of course not…" But he's right to ask. I did it once before.

"Nathan," Beatrix snaps. She shakes her head, her face paling even more. "She didn't. He was admitted three hours ago. Motorcycle accident," the words break in her mouth as she says them.

My legs are moving before I know it. Beatrix and Nathan clamor behind me. I'm inside my car, the familiar black and chrome detailing blurring in my sight. Warmth fills my eyes. My hands grip at the wheel to steady themselves.

The driver's door opens. "Get out. I'll drive," Beatrix is saying. She helps me unbuckle, holds my arms steady, and gets me to the other side of the car. She's backing out before I make sense of what just happened, before I can even get my seatbelt clicked in. "Tell me where to go."

"Lime Street," I manage.

Nathan taps lightly on the window with the back of his knuckles.

Beatrix rolls it down.

"I know where it is, just follow me."

"How do you—"

Nathan grins. "Safety first, bitches." His motorcycle purrs to life outside of my vehicle.

Beatrix whips the car out of the driveway and follows Nathan.

My head rolls on the seat. Images flash through my head. No information. No "stable," confirmation from the hospital.

Nothing. I imagine him wrapped head to toe. I imagine missing limbs. I imagine blood on his skin, the site of the accident. Was someone else involved? Did he get pinned at the site? Did he just lose control?

Darkness and trees dissolve into a black mass outside the window. The car dips in and out of darkness and streetlights, never out of range of the rumble of Nathan's bike. The hospital meets us as a beacon of sterile white light in the short, salt-covered forest around it. We're parked. We walk in. The world seems to move around me, unwilling to let me take a moment to recover my breath, to ground myself in the reality of what's happening. Nathan is stopped by security for a pocketknife; he tells us to go on without him and says he'll catch up. Beatrix ushers me forward. She speaks to the front desk. They ask who we are. Beatrix explains in a voice like rock candy. Sweet. Hard. All edges and angles.

The nurse asks for a moment, leaves the desk.

Beatrix turns to me and says something.

I don't hear her.

I watch the nurse disappear behind the corner and into the double-door entry to the emergency room. She returns. She tells Bea something else I can't hear.

Nathan asks a question behind me.

I keep staring at those doors.

"He's in surgery right now." It's the third time someone's said that. Beatrix shakes me. "We have to wait."

"After three hours?" My stomach twists again.

"We have to wait, Katrina." Again. "Come on, let's sit down." Bea's hands are on my arms. The cold floor beneath my boots. The faint smell of antiseptic as we sit. The sound of the plastic material stretching beneath us. Distant beeps. A phone call, somewhere. Nurses chatter.

Time passes unforgivably slow. I drift in and out of what can barely be considered *consciousness*. My mind plays tricks on me. Every time the door clicks behind us, I think someone is calling my name. I think *Corbin* is calling my name. My head rests on Beatrix's shoulders. Nathan leaves once. He returns with a dollar store blanket and drapes it over Beatrix and me. I watch him flirt with the nurses at the front desk, hear Beatrix swear at his blatant disrespect, and Nathan's witty comeback about making the best out of a shitty situation.

I dream I'm on the back of Corbin's bike. I dream of the crash, of being pulled away from him violently, being dumped across the road. I wake from a falling sensation with a hard jerk.

Beatrix strokes my hair.

Why did you leave him on that rooftop?

Sterile silence.

The rise and fall of Beatrix's chest as she breathes.

The sound of Nathan's leather riding boots pacing the floor.

If you would have stayed, this wouldn't have happened.

Maybe if you would have gone with him this morning, this wouldn't have happened.

Then, that dreaded thought.

What if he dies?

You would have never had the chance to tell him how you really feel, how it's not his fault that you tend to run away, that you want to overcome the wounds from your past so you can love him like he deserves.

I'm not even sure why he wants my love. He's rich and handsome. He could have anyone he wanted.

Why me, Ben? Why did you choose me? I ask Beatrix what he sees in me.

"You're the one thing he can't have," Beatrix says. "You're elusive. You have nothing, but in his eyes, it's like you have everything. True freedom. Sometimes I think he's jealous. Maybe he's just trying to learn."

My heart keeps twisting in awful, terrible ways.

I wonder if I'll ever get to kiss him again.

"I love him, Bea."

"I know, Katrina," she whispers. "He does too."

"What if… What if…"

I feel like a child.

"Don't even go there," Nathan snaps. "He'll be fine."

Somehow, that's harder to believe than I'd like it to be.

Chapter Twenty-One

CORBIN

Everything hurts. My eyes are burning and dry. My throat is coarse and sore. My back. And oh, *god*, my leg. Fire shoots through my veins the second I try to move. My neck, my head, my arms—all the way down to my fingertips. My stiff fingertips. I can't move my hands. Something is moaning in the distance, and it sounds like a wild animal, two seconds away from death.

I try to open my eyes.

What's happening?

White blinds me.

Where is that animal?

Vibration. Pain, endlessly. Another moan.

Oh god, it's me. *What happened?*

Someone is speaking. Words. Sentences, I can't make sense of.

"…for the next few hours. You'll need someone who can help you. Your recovery won't be easy…but…"

Where am I?

"Your friends are outside. Beatrix, Nathan, and Katrina. We can't let them in just yet…"

Flashes return.

The screech of my tires. The beams of two, massive headlights. The crunch of gravel. The world spinning, over and over and over and over. Pain. *Cracking* in my ears. The crunching of metal.

"Honestly, you're lucky you're alive."

I try again to peel my eyelids back.

"You were in a crash."

"Katrina…"

"We'll allow them in shortly. We need to monitor your vitals a little longer." The nurse places a piece of white plastic in my numb hand, wrapping the cord around the hospital bed siding. "If you need more medicine, you can click the red button on the top here, and it will administer a small dose every few hours."

I click the button, and the nurse gives me a sympathetic look. "Not quite yet. Get some rest. When you wake up, your friends will be here. We'll be here too, if you need anything at all."

I try to nod, but I don't move at all.

MY SURROUNDINGS RETURN TO ME, slowly at first. A dull, monotone beeping. The smell of bleach and antiseptic. The quiet roll of wheels on linoleum. People murmur in a dreary conversation, somewhere nearby. I listen as best I can, but I can only make out the vibrato of their voices. Familiar pitches. The sound of home. Beatrix and Nathan are muttering back and forth, a twinge of sass ever-lingering on their inaudible words.

Fingers are brushing the hair out of my face. Gently. Tentatively.

I open my eyes.

White glares back down.

"Hey," a whisper.

I turn towards it.

Katrina gazes at me with all her soft features—her curly orange hair, her golden-brown eyes, her petal-pink lips. The freckles on her cheeks dance as she forces a small, sad smile. Tears shimmer in the corners of her eyes. "I thought you left."

I scoff, which only results in a shockwave of pain.

I try to reach for Katrina, but my hand is stiff, and something pulls tight. I look. I'm hooked up to multiple wires from multiple places; there's an IV in the top of my hand.

"Don't move," she whispers. A tear slides down her face.

"Do I look that bad?" I manage in a coarse, dry voice.

Katrina nods, fully crying now. Her face wrinkles with emotion, splotches with pink. Her fingers stroke the top of one of my hands—which I only now realize she's holding. It's warped in a cast, immobile to me. I look at my other hand, which is bandaged firmly and in a brace; the button the nurse gave me in on the bed beside my hand. It must've fallen out while I slept.

"You shattered your leg and broke bones in both of your hands. The doctors say you walked away with minimal injuries, given the accident you were in. The driver who hit you was drunk. He crossed the yellow line."

Sounds right.

"They've already cleaned out most of the gravel from your road rash burns… They said you were unconscious when they brought you in. Passed out from the pain," Beatrix says over Katrina's shoulder, ever the stoic in moments of crisis. I wish I could learn that from her, but instead, I feel hot tears spilling over my face. The pain is incredible, more than I can fathom. Even breathing makes the bones in my chest ache with soreness and exhaustion.

"Do you have any plans for what happens after you get released?" Beatrix asks.

I shake my head. *Of course not. I haven't even been able to think past the pain I'm currently in right now.* But she brings up a good point. I'm not worried about the bill. Hell, I'm not even worried about pressing charges against whoever hit me. I don't need the money. I'm sure the driver was arrested on the site of the accident; that's punishment enough, if you ask me.

"I can help," Katrina says. She looks up at Beatrix as if she's looking for approval or a final say, as if I need permission from Beatrix to do things.

"He can stay with us at the rental if—"

"No," Katrina says firmly, her voice a little quiet. "I can look after him at my place."

I watch her.

Katrina's eyes are tired but determined. If Beatrix only knew her well enough, she wouldn't have even offered. Because there's one thing I know for a fact about Katrina: There is no one else she trusts with my wellbeing, especially after knowing my family. The only place she'll let me be vulnerable is at the mercy of her own hands.

THE HOSPITAL RELEASES ME AFTER four days. And for those four days, Katrina is at my bedside day and night. She brings me Chinese takeout and hand-feeds me after my first and only attempt at lifting a plastic fork in my right hand. I spilled the whole forkfuls all across the pristine, white hospital sheet, splashing sauce all over my face in the process. When Katrina walked in on the sight, she burst into laughter then forbade me from ever doing that again.

The hospital staff carts me out in a wheelchair on the day I leave. Katrina and Nathan help me into Katrina's car, careful not to knock the bulky cast on my right leg.

When we pull up to the little white cottage by the sea, Beatrix rolls a brand new matte black and leather wheelchair to the side of the car. "We took some creative liberty to snazz up your new wheels. Hope you like it."

I laugh at the ridiculousness of what she's just said and study the wheelchair a little closer.

"Genuine-*fucking*-leather, bro. Merry Christmas, cause that's all you're getting out of me for the rest of the goddamn year," Nathan says. He stands, arms crossed, looking a little too proud about the wheelchair.

On the front, they've ironed a huge compass on the seat. On the backrest, a set of angel wings. Nathan spins it around for me to see the back. *KEEP ROLLIN FAM* is printed on the back with edgy, gothic text.

"We almost put *Famine,* but Nate thought this was funnier."

Nathan laughs again under his breath.

"It was his joke, by the way," Beatrix explains, deadpan.

I look at the two of them, gratitude swelling in my chest. I open my mouth to speak, but Beatrix cuts me off quickly.

"Please don't cry," she says.

I laugh instead. "Thank you. I love it."

After helping me inside, Beatrix and Nate stay for a round of cards with Katrina and me. When my eyelids start getting heavy, Beatrix collectively calls it a night for us and ushers Nathan towards the door. She orders me to get some rest—shooting a charged look at Katrina as if to say, *Don't keep him up!*—then the door slams. It auto-locks behind them.

I'm left at the dinner table with Katrina and the cards that are still splayed four ways across the light, wood table. I reach to collect the cards, but Katrina places a gentle hand on mine.

"Let me," she says. Katrina sweeps up the plastic black and gold playing cards and slides them back into the sleeve. "I can sleep on the couch, if you need the room."

I shake my head.

Katrina's warm eyes settle on me. "I thought I'd lost you. Emotionally at first," she whispers, "then, *for real* there for a second."

The dim light of her living room and kitchen paint her a shade of honey-orange, hair dripping in curls over her shoulders. The night sky of freckles on her chest spins as she moves, dazzling me in new ways. She catches me staring and tilts her head in curiosity.

I breathe deep then say, "I'm sorry, Katrina."

"Why are you apologizing?"

"I should have been more careful."

"Accidents happen. Especially to the wild." Pointed words, coming from her.

"Are you telling me to settle down?" I ask, raising an eyebrow.

Her expression becomes uneasy. A pinch in her brows, a hair brushed behind her ear. Her mouth works as she searches for words. "No, of course not… That was just…such a close call."

"I know."

Katrina watches me again. "Do you think you could sleep?"

I nod. "Painkillers do wonders for sleep."

"C'mon." Katrina stands finally, walks around the back of my wheelchair, then rolls me towards her bedroom. Her silence is so loud, so hard to wrap my head around. She's usually quiet, yes, but this is something new. Concern laces the edges of the space between our words. I've never felt her concern before. Not like this.

Chapter Twenty-Two

KATRINA

I TRY MY BEST TO sleep, but it eludes me, tiptoeing around the corners of my mind, poking at every thought so they stay on topic. On Corbin. In a desperate attempt to think of other things, I slip out of bed, leaving him there alone; his shallow breaths raise his chest faintly under the covers. At the end of the bed, his cast is propped up on every spare pillow we found in my rental.

I breathe deep. I know I won't really get my mind off him, but I need an escape. After nearly a week in the hospital, my nerves are completely fried. I feel as if I haven't had fresh air in my lungs in over a month. Pulling on some soft pajamas and a set of flip-flops, I head outside and cross the empty beach road over to the beach.

The night air is sticky in my lungs. The sound of cicadas singing fills the darkness. Then, the rush of the ocean.

I sit on the boardwalk, right at the end, and put my feet on the steps leading down into the sand. I lean against the wood railing and close my eyes and listen. The ocean breathes in the distance, steady, loud. I try to clear my mind, try to focus on being *here and now*.

I've taken time off work this past week to look after Corbin. After dipping into my savings for a few days, I'd told Corbin I had to go back in otherwise I wouldn't be able to foot my rent this month. Of course, without much of a surprise to me or anyone, Corbin offered to cover any expenses required of me while looking after him and pay back what I've already spent. Like his own on-call nurse. The thought makes me queasy. It's not that I want the money, but rather that I need it. But having him lay down as much cash as I need makes me feel obligated to do whatever he asks, even though I know he would never be unreasonable.

I glance at my phone to check the time. 4:43 A.M. My regular shift would start this morning at ten. If I went back now, I'd be lucky to manage even two more hours—between tossing and turning through all of my worries and then waking at eight to prepare for the day.

Opening my texts, I scroll through my contacts until I find my text string with Jackson. I look at the last conversation we had, lit with abrasive blue and white light.

JACKSON

YOU KNOW THAT GUY WHO SHOWED UP AT THE DINER LOOKING FOR ME?

YEAH. WHAT ABOUT HIM?

IS HE GIVING YOU TROUBLE?

NO. WE WERE SERIOUS WHEN WE WERE BACK IN CHICAGO. HE WAS ABOUT TO PROPOSE BEFORE I MOVED DOWN HERE, AND WE'VE BEEN TALKING. WE'VE BEEN MORE OR LESS DATING AGAIN.

HE GOT IN A MOTORCYCLE WRECK LAST NIGHT.

I'M AT THE HOSPITAL WITH HIM RIGHT NOW.

IS THERE SOMEONE WHO CAN COVER MY SHIFT TOMORROW? I DON'T KNOW HOW LONG I'LL BE HERE TONIGHT.

OMG, IS HE OKAY??

DON'T WORRY ABOUT IT, KAT. WE'LL GET IT COVERED.

If there was such a thing as a *best boss* award, Jackson would've won it a long time ago. I guess I can't entirely lend it to him as a boss, but rather too to the friendship we've developed over the years. It's not unusual for us to text outside of work, or maybe even grab the occasional beer. That's all thanks to the small-town, family-run business. Otherwise, it probably would've been raising eyebrows.

I type up a small message, telling him I can resume working half-shifts. I don't want to rely completely on Corbin for income. It makes what I've made here—my job, my rental, my life—feel as if it's all been for nothing, that I hadn't achieved anything besides running back into his arms. I still need that sense of normalcy to keep my feet grounded, I realize. Not to mention, I genuinely miss my regulars too… Not something I ever thought would cross my mind.

My message *blips* onto my screen with a subtle haptic in my palm. I click my phone locked and stare into the blackness ahead of me until my eyes readjust. Very faintly, the waterline is visible. There's a vague grayish line that grows and fades where the water breaks on the shore in tiny waves. Beyond that, the sea disappears into the sky. It's impossible to tell the two apart.

Above, there's a swath of stars that spreads to the far corners of the sky. There are so many that, as I lean my head back to look, I simply give up and stand, walk down to the beach and lay flat on the sand. From my position on the ground, I can see at least half of the night sky, yet my eyes *still* don't feel big enough—or reach far enough—to fully appreciate the vastness of the expanse above me.

It's breathtaking.

Just like my first night here, I'm reminded how much I love the stars. How limitless it looks up there. How small I feel down here. How insignificant it makes my problems feel. They will all resolve… eventually. And eventually, when they do, the stars will still be up in the sky, everlasting.

As I lay, as I breathe, as I try my best to meditate on the size of *me* and the size of *that,* even more stars start to peek out from the spaces between. It paints its own beach in the sky, with the Milky Way posing as the sea foam on the edge of the water.

I wish I could get lost in those stars, just float endlessly, forever.

I have felt as if I've been fighting the sea itself, inside my mind. Every handful of years, something new. The whirlwind of my childhood, then meeting Corbin just after I turned twenty-four. The push and pull of our relationship, the hot and cold of our high-strung emotions and fights.

Why won't you let me love you? Why can't you let me in?

He would never understand. How could he possibly understand?

Every new pull from him, a push away from me. The closer he tried to get, the further I drew back. Just like the ocean. And just like the ocean, it pulled every piece of my façade apart until finally, there was nothing left but…me.

After I left—that's when I realized. I was running from him because I didn't believe he could love me. Then, here, after meeting Jackson and my coworkers—after they loved me in their own way, I started to consider that maybe Corbin was being truthful. Maybe he was in love with me; maybe he still *is*. Because it's true—there's nothing that I have that could benefit him but that. There is nothing he stands to gain from our relationship, besides my love.

The idea was so foreign for a long time. Now, I'm only beginning to grasp at the frayed edges of the concept.

If I had just let him in. If I had just let him shower me with love, like he wanted to. If only I hadn't pulled away, over and over again.

Maybe none of this would have happened.

But maybe, just maybe, I would've never got here—mentally—if I never would have left. I would have never known true friendship. I would have never known the deep-cut scars on my bones and on my heart. (The sixteen-hour car ride here let me unearth those.) I would have never been able to even partially begin to patch those wounds. (The ocean helped me heal those.) Which, maybe, means it's possible I could've never loved him the way I was meant to. Limitlessly, endlessly, like the night sky above.

Maybe I would've never had the chance to love him right.

And now I've been given not only a second chance, but a *third* chance.

They say third time's a charm, I think to myself listlessly.

The sand crunches behind my head as I turn to gaze down the dark beach. I can't see much, but the action makes my eyes heavy, as if I could fall asleep if I just got comfortable enough.

You could sleep out here. Waking to the sunrise wouldn't be so bad.

I tuck the idea away for another time; it's something that I think would be more fun with Corbin, with four armfuls of blankets and two bottles of wine. In time. All in good time.

Chapter Twenty-Three

CORBIN

WHEN I FINALLY WAKE, KATRINA is gone. Pain crashes back into me, the second after I realize this. I can barely even crane my neck to look at the crumpled sheets beside me. When I do, I find a small note on her pillow. I pick it up.

On it, Katrina's neat, small handwriting scrawls in deep blue ink:

I'm working this morning at the diner. I'm only working a half-shift, so I'll be back at two. If you need anything at all, just call me. I'll come straight back.

I lift my head to search the room for a clock. There's a small, analog, black and red one sitting on her dresser. It reads 1:58 P.M.

She must've guessed as much. With the painkillers I'm on, it would be pointless for her to sit around and stare at the wall while I sleep the day away. Still, part of me wishes she would've done it. I would've done it for her. I don't think I could've done anything *besides* watch her sleep, if the roles were reversed. To make sure her breath still lifted her chest. To make sure her eyes still opened again.

I tuck that small heartache away into a deep fold in my mind. I can't think of things like that. I'm lucky to be here. I'm lucky Katrina *cared enough* to show up at the hospital before *my* eyes had even opened. Maybe this was all just a test of hers. Maybe this was her way of saying, *I will love you, but you have to let me be free, too.* It sounds about right. I *should* give her some freedom. I don't doubt she'd come home five minutes after I made a call, either. She may be flighty, but her loyalty is starting to show.

That doesn't stop me from wanting her here, now, though.

As if to answer my thoughts, the front door creaks open. The sounds of Katrina coming in fill the little rental cottage— the jangle of her car key and pepper spray key chain, the sound of her dropping her small wedge boots onto the floor, the *thwump* of her purse hitting the kitchen chair.

I can't help but smile. It's the same pattern, the same routine she had back in Chicago, when she would come stay at my flat. Some things have changed, but not everything.

The kitchen sink squeaks and hisses. The soap pump squirts noisily.

Funny how much you can hear when there's nothing more you want in life but to watch those events unfold.

Funny how, even though you know time is moving, sometimes it stands still.

The moments between her coming through the door and arriving in the bedroom feel like an eternity. When she finally does, I feel as if the sky has cleared of a relentless storm and the sun is finally shining again.

Katrina's wild hair is pulled back in a slick ponytail; her face is paler than usual, with rings starting beneath her eyes. She isn't wearing makeup this morning, something I've come to learn as her lack of energy rather than confidence in her looks. She must not have slept much last night. I wonder how much of that was my fault.

"How are you feeling?" she asks me.

"Painful," I say.

She grimaces, as if she expected the response. She walks over and sits beside me. "Is there anything I can do to help?"

I try to shake my head, but the bones in my neck are too sore, so I just tell her *no* instead. I wish there was. I wish her kisses could banish all the pain from my bones. I wish she could press her lips across every inch of my body and heal me just with her affection. But no. Healing takes time. I should know.

Katrina's fingertips trace the side of my face. She runs them along my jawline, scratching her long nails through my beard. My eyes flit closed; I forgot just *how good* that felt. "How about a shave?" she asks.

I nod, helpless at her fingertips.

She helps me out of bed, slowly, carefully, and into my wheelchair. As soon as my leg is below my heart, I feel pressure build there, behind the pain. Katrina wheels me into her master bathroom and digs through the sink drawers. Makeup and other miscellaneous items clatter and roll around as she searches. Finally, she procures a small plastic box of razors, something, it seems, she's held onto all this way away from Chicago. She flips the cap open and draws one out. "It's been a while," she says, looking at the silver edge of the blade thoughtfully.

"I've missed it," I whisper.

Katrina's golden-brown eyes turn on me, sharp as the razor in her hand.

My stomach does a little somersault at the sight of her. I lift my chin in an invitation. Katrina locks the wheels on my chairs and slips her legs through the handles of the wheelchair until she's able to sit straight on my lap, the warmth of her settling through my hips.

"Is this okay?" she asks.

I nod. "I'll tell you if it gets to hurting."

"I don't have any shaving cream…"

"Go easy."

"You know I always do."

I close my eyes as Katrina lifts my chin a little further. She plants a gentle kiss on my chin, then on my throat. She runs the flat side of the blade across my skin. She takes her time, and I focus on the shifting of her weight on my lap, the way she turns my head meticulously, the way the blade glides effortlessly across my skin with the softest *scratching* sound as it cuts through my coarse hair.

When Katrina finishes, she places the razor on the counter behind us with a quiet *clink* and holds my face in her hand. Ever so slowly, she places her lips on mine.

I let my hands cradle her shoulders, then run the length of her back. They settle on her hips, scrunching the fabric of her maxi dress in my hands.

Katrina deepens the kiss; her mouth tastes like lipstick and flowers. As the kiss gets heated, she grabs the hem of my shirt and pulls it over my head. She's left staring, heavy-lidded at the rise and fall of my chest and the ball-chain necklace that holds the engagement ring I bought for her. She's never seen it before now, I realize. Only the impression of it.

"Is that…"

"The same one," I finish for her.

Silence.

Then, slowly, "You never took it off…"

"Why would I?"

Her eyes find mine, settle there, leave a white spot in my vision like the sun itself. The room moves around me—moves around *her*.

"I still love you, Katrina."

Her face goes distant, like it always does when I say those words.

"You loved me then, didn't you?" I prod.

"Of course, I…"

My hand finds the ring on my chest, and Katrina flinches back. But her legs are trapped, and she can't move as gracefully or quickly as she needs to to escape me or this conversation. My other hand holds her leg still. "What is it you're not telling me?"

Katrina stares at my hand on my chest, the ring underneath.

"Why is it so hard for you to see that I love you?"

"It's not, Ben," she says, voice stiff and unrelenting to the emotion showing on her face. "I know you love me, and I love you too…but—"

"But *what*, Katrina? Am I not enough? Did I not tell you what you wanted to hear? What did I do wrong?" The words tumble, one after another, until all my insecurities are laid bare before her.

"It's not *that*." Her eyes fix me with a glare, but tears threaten the corners of them. One slips over, racing down her freckled cheek. Her next words are a whisper, "Why would you think that?"

"Because, Katrina, every time we get close to something good, you run away. What are you running from, if it's not me?"

"You wouldn't understand," she says, eyes falling to her lap, to where my hand has stayed steady on her leg.

"Try me."

Katrina's eyes close and the tears fall freely. "It's silly."

"Nothing that made you run for this long is silly," I assure her. "*Try me*."

"I grew up in the system," her voice like smoke.

That's when it hits me. Of course I wouldn't understand. She knew from day one, that *that* was the one thing I could never wrap my head around. The boy with a mother and father, with a circle of friends, with anything I could want for on a silver platter. I could never even begin to comprehend the life she's been through.

"I don't know my parents," she says. "Each foster family passed me off." She sniffles.

That's not silly, I think. I try to encourage the words from my mouth, but I remain silent, unable to respond outwardly, even though my mind is a bullet train with no rails, no destination.

"Say something," she cries. "Please."

I pull Katrina against my chest and hold her. "I love you, Katrina. All of you. They don't know what they're missing."

"A flighty waitress one step away from a track record," she blubbers against my chest. Snot and tears wet my skin.

"You're fearless. And you're free. You can go *anywhere*, see *anything*. You live life in the moment. I wish I could be more like you, in that way." I hope my words aren't harming her, and inwardly I walk a fine line between telling myself to shut up and worrying that saying nothing in this moment is worse than my poor attempt at reassuring her. I hold her until she stops crying, until her warm skin cools again and her chest stills against mine.

When she sits back up straight, she doesn't look me in the eye. She takes a damp wash cloth and cleans the stray hairs off of my chest, trying—visibly—to ignore the giant rock in her way.

"I can take it off, if you want," I tell her, reaching to lift the chain.

She pauses. "No." She brushes a hair from her cheek. "You're entitled to how you feel."

I want to thank her, but again, the sight of her tears and her defeat renders me silent.

"I just need time," she says finally. She stands then kneels, unlocks my wheels, then leaves me in the bathroom alone.

Chapter Twenty-Four

CORBIN

THE NEXT FEW DAYS PASS in a semi-comfortable silence. At first, Katrina is cold and distant and helps me without exchanging words. The following day, she looks at me again, her eyes curious of *me*—such a strange thing to witness. It's as if she's trying to understand why I, of all people, stayed. Then, she warms up again, ever-slowly—touching my shoulders as she passes me, leaving kisses on the top of my head. That's when the silence becomes comfortable again.

It occurs to me that maybe this is what I never offered her. Maybe allowing her the time to return to *me* is what was lacking in our relationship before. I was so busy chasing after her the second she left, that of *course* she would feel clobbered and run faster. I just wish she would've told me sooner. If she had, maybe I would've been able to grasp the situation better.

Recovery moves slower than I'd like, and the weeks turn into months. June turns into August. What I thought was the peak of summer in the early weeks of April when my friends and I first rolled into town downright proves me wrong. That was just the trial run of summer. Now the rays of sunlight are supercharged with heat that cuts through windows. Katrina keeps the blinds drawn to save money on her electric bill, and I wonder if Nathan and Beatrix are doing the same just to stay cool.

My friends stop over a few nights every week, and the four of us always gather around Katrina's small kitchen table to play a few rounds of rummy. Nathan tells us about his bad luck job hunting, and Beatrix about her exponentially good luck in the same endeavors. Beatrix had secured a job at a watersports company that gave tours around the island, and Nathan (on Bea's good word) managed a part-time position at the same job. Beatrix glows every time she talks about her job—and the job glows on her—her skin darkening ever so slightly with a healthy tan. Nathan, on the other hand, is more often red and angry from it.

Eventually, I lose the braces on my hands and graduate to crutches and manage to do more things on my own. Still, when Katrina offers to help me shower or shave, I am more than happy to let her.

Our life becomes steady for once, with Katrina flitting in and out of my days, leaving kisses on the top of my head, on my eyelids when I sleep. Every time I try to reach out and hold her still, though, she seems to pull away. Metaphorically. The nights we have sex—I beg her to stay with me and let me hold her, but she always says she needs a minute, leaves the bedroom, then steals into the night. The only time I asked where she goes to, she told me she simply needed a moment to look at the stars, to ground herself. I let her. Each time, she comes back.

It's easier than it's been in a long time. Not trying to hold her back has given her the freedom she needs, from what I can see.

Tonight, when she comes home from her evening shift, I greet her at the door.

Katrina smiles up at me shyly. "Hi," she says.

"Welcome home, Freckles."

Her face flushes lightly, making her complexion warm and rosy.

"Dinner's in the kitchen. Takeout."

Katrina laughs at this. "I thought maybe we could cook together tonight. It is my Friday after all."

"Sorry. I think you'll like this place, though." I use my crutches to hobble into the kitchen as Katrina locks the door and drops her stuff on one of the chairs. Instead of following me into the kitchen, though, she stays in the living room.

The TV clicks on.

"The tropical depression we've been watching is expected to turn into a hurricane here within a week. We're looking at landfall a week after that. Possibly category one; possibly category two. All of that is going to depend on the way the storm gains strength as it sits over the warm water in the coming days…"

I turn to look at Katrina.

The TV screen illuminates her in a ghostly blue hue.

"So what does that mean for us?"

The TV continues to ramble on.

"Well, it depends. If it's a category two…" Katrina's eyes fall on my leg. "Evacuation, maybe. We just have to watch and see what the storm looks like as it gets closer. But with your injuries, it's not a good idea to stick around."

"Are you trying to get rid of me?" I cock an eyebrow at her.

Her lips press together. "Hurricanes can be dangerous."

I shrug and smile. "I like a little danger."

"You've had more than enough danger for the rest of the year, Ace." Katrina shuts the TV off and joins me in the kitchen. She unpacks the brown paper bag of Chinese food and sets the food on the table. "We'll play it by ear."

THE FOLLOWING DAYS DRAG BY. With my hands finally free and one leg back in order, I spend my days walking around the house with my crutches to regain some strength. I find myself in front of the TV one too many times, watching anxiously as forecasters showed colorful spaghetti models and the storm growing in size and speed. Without much to do outside besides sweating to death in my leg cast and black clothes, I end up calling Nathan over for the day to pass the time while Katrina's at work.

I open the door to greet Nathan; he beams back at me with a sunburned smile. "Looks like you're living in a cave in there! Holy shit." He barges in, steps back, then lifts his black Ray-Ban sunglasses into his white-blond hair. The scent of sunblock, seawater, and sweat follows him in. "Lookin' good, hot stuff. Could use a bit of a tan, though, if you ask me."

"You could use a little *less* of a tan. Honestly, Nate, you look like a lobster."

"It's not my fucking fault. The boss had us working all day at the Ritz looking after some company's whole team. They had us lugging kayaks up and down the beach nonstop. Idiots didn't even know how to get inside the damn kayaks, either."

I can't help but chuckle. I've heard plenty of stories like this—and after a quick glance at Nathan's black shorts in search of saltwater stains and finding them—I'm sure he spent his day waist-deep trying to help tourists into those said kayaks.

"I gotta find a different job, dude. This is killing me."

"Have you thought about one of the local restaurants?" I follow Nathan over to the couch where he collapses and wipes the sweat from his forehead.

"Yeah, I have, but hell no. The food industry is where I draw the line."

I sit on the other end of the couch and watch Nathan revel in the darkness of the living room. I'll admit, even though I like the sun, the sweat that forms after a shy two minutes outside here does me in. I've spent as much time as I possibly can out of the heat. Once I ditch the cast, I anticipate getting some late fall swimming in, since I've heard the Florida heat lasts well into the final weeks of October.

"I'm actually thinking about dabbling in the arts," Nathan says with an exhausted *puff* of air. "I know it won't make money right away, but hey, why not? There are tons of rich people dying to spend their art on contemporary splatter *art*."

Nathan makes quotations with his fingers for the last word. "How hard can that possibly be?"

"Supplies," I offer.

"I'm saving up some cash."

I shrug. "Time. Studio space. Fuck, Nathan, just whatever you do, don't make them keep our deposit."

"I won't, I won't!" He raises his hands in mock surrender. "I don't know, but I'm hoping to scout out a couple galleries here in a week or so when the rush slows down at work."

I motion towards the TV. "You heard about the storm that's brewing?"

"Yep," Nathan says. His eyes go sarcastically wide, and he runs both his hands through his wind-whipped hair. "It's a little scary, I'm not gonna lie. The guys at work keep joking about a hurricane party, but I don't know. It's different when you're watching it, landlocked, sixteen hours in every direction. Being this close to it's kinda wild."

I nod in agreement. Honestly, I feel the same way. Ever since Katrina brought it up, I haven't been able to shake a sinking feeling of dread. Part of me wants to up and leave. Truth is, if it were Beatrix, Nathan, and me down in Miami, we would've hit the road at the first wind we caught of the storm. Motorcycles and hurricanes don't mix. I sigh. "Katrina seems to think a category one isn't a big deal."

Nathan rolls his eyes and picks up his phone. "Yeah, ninety-five mile-per-hour winds don't sound terrifying at all. The ocean is like *two* streets over from this place."

"You don't have to tell me."

"God! Katrina's crazy, man. I'd be out of here tomorrow if you weren't here. No way in hell I'm leaving her to look after you in a storm."

"Hurricane party at the rental?" I joke. I raise an eyebrow at Nathan.

The look on his face is less *joking* and more *considering*.

"Hell, why not? If we're gonna stay, let's ride it out together." Nathan pauses, lost in thought. "Bea and I can stock up on supplies. Should we count on Katrina?"

"I mean, I'm not leaving her here by herself if we're doing this, so yeah." I fish my wallet out of my pocket and hand Nathan a fifty and a twenty. "Stock up on some beer while you're at it."

"Hell yeah," Nathan says. "Will do."

Chapter Twenty-Five

KATRINA

THE HEAT OF THE DAY beats into my back as I fill my car up with gas. Two cars wait behind mine. I sigh at the rush, defeated. The storm has grown significantly worse overnight, and the regular updates on the storm have pulled my mind off work and my relationship with Corbin and put it straight on the safety of me and Corbin and his friends instead.

With the hurricane now approaching at a category two and expected to make landfall as a category three, tensions have run high all over the island. The last time a hurricane made a direct hit on this area in Florida was Hurricane Dora back in 1964. It's a local legend of a storm here, as most hurricanes ride the Gulf Stream up and away from Northeast Florida.

My trunk is packed with bottled water and boiled peanuts and apples and bananas and canned corn and green beans. I tried to find some shelf-stable junk food to add to the stash, since in reality, I'm buying for not only Corbin and myself but Nathan and Beatrix too. Chips, bagged popcorn, Nutty Buddy's, and Zebra Cakes. I went out of my way to grab a gluten-free vegan stash of knockoff Pringles and Girl Scout cookies. Corbin told me before I did this run that he already spotted Nathan seventy dollars for alcohol.

I grab my receipt and pocket it and climb back in the car. Ice-cold AC blasts my face and arms and blows through my hair, making loose curls tickle my face.

I don't hate the idea of a hurricane party; it sounds a little fun. But the fact that Corbin is still hobbling around in crutches with a bulky cast on his leg worries me. Any flooding or downed trees—or walls inside of a house for that matter— become nearly fatal, as if they weren't already dangerous as is.

As I drive home—now, with all the preparations for the storm *mostly* in order—I'm able to think more clearly about how things have been between Corbin and myself. Waking up next to him every morning for the past couple of months has worn down on my walls, day after day. Now that he knows— at least surface level, what I went through as a kid—he's backed off a little. It's given me room to breathe, to think. It's helped me grasp the situation better, helped me know that he has no ulterior motive in pursuing me. He's simply in it for *me*. It sounds silly, but I've even gone as far as faking my period to get out of sex, and even then, he's nothing but understanding. He's not in it for the sex, as good as it is.

I've been trying to open up more. I've been wanting to tell him more, to sit down and have time to tell Corbin about each and every one of my foster parents. I want to make sure he knows the stories that I know so well, that I've spent countless hours unraveling in my head to understand *why* I make the decisions I do, why I react the way I react. The more he knows about what it's like inside my head, the more he'll understand who I am.

But that takes time.

Time, that I've been wasting at the diner.

Time that is quickly running out with every second the hurricane is approaching.

I'm still not sure if Corbin will actually decide to stay.

If he leaves, I'm not sure how I'll respond.

I could go with him, yes. But would I?

Or would I decide to plant my feet no matter how hard he pulls my hand?

My mind races with these thoughts until the moment I pull into the driveway and see Nathan's fire-red motorcycle parked in the spot Corbin used to park his. I shoot Nathan a quick text—since both his contact and Bea's are in my phone after Corbin's accident—and ask for a hand with bringing in the snacks. Nathan texts back almost immediately and tells me we'll be taking the snacks to their rental, so we should leave them in my car.

I sigh and lean my head back against the headrest.

Whether I want to or not, the decisions I'll need to make over the oncoming storm are growing ever closer, faster and faster. My head spins like the approaching vortex. I take a few deep breaths to steady myself before I step out of the car. I leave it unlocked, knowing I'll probably be back in no time to haul Corbin over to his rental with his friends. Besides, if that plan fails, I'll have to retrieve anything and everything made of chocolate out of the car in ten minutes tops, lest it melts completely in the evening heat.

Stepping inside, cold washes over me. It smells of popcorn and beer, and I find Corbin and Nathan sitting in front of the TV with several open beer cans and the weather channel playing on full blast.

Corbin looks at me with bleary eyes and a silly grin.

"I don't think he's supposed to be drinking, Nathan." I turn my eyes on him.

Nathan visibly shrinks back. "He just had one. The rest were mine. I forgot about the painkillers, and he forgot to mention them…"

I sigh, again, and make a mental note that Nathan is in no way, shape, or form capable of looking after Corbin in recovery. "Get out," I tell Nathan.

"Hey, look, it's not my fault! He didn't *tell* me."

"Of course he didn't tell you, he's literally *drugged*," I snap. "Out. Now. I'll have him text you later."

"Okay, fine." Nathan stands, gathers his trash, and tosses it before heading out. He slams the door behind him for good measure.

I roll my eyes and follow him out to retrieve the meltable snacks in my car.

Nathan revs his engine as he walks his motorcycle past me. "I didn't do it on purpose."

"I know," I say as I pull the bags out of the car, "but you still did it." I fix him with another cold glare, and he rolls his eyes back at me.

Nathan tucks a bright red bandanna over his nose and idles beside me a moment longer. His lime-green eyes peer back, devoid of any readable emotion.

"What?" I say, a little too sharply. Plastic bags crinkle in my arms as I shut my car door and lock it. My car beeps twice then leaves us in an awkward silence.

"I want to be friends. I'm sorry I screwed up." His voice is muffled. "Give me another chance. I swear I want what's best for him. Clearly, that's *you* taking care of him. Please," he stresses the word, "give me another chance to make it up to you. I really want to be on good terms."

It's the most honest I think anyone's ever been with me, and it immediately earns him back some points from his dumb stunt at the bar and *this*. I sigh heavily—wondering if I'm running out of breath for the day—and say, "Got it. Fine. Clean slate."

Nathan lifts a pinky finger at me. "Pinky swear?"

I pause before I move, consider this truce before I make it. *What a dumb way to seal a deal.* "Fine," I say again. I lift a hand—which is inconveniently full of grocery store bags— and offer him my pinky finger. "Pinky swear."

Nathan's eyes crinkle with delight. He grabs my pinky in his and squeezes. "See ya round, Freckles."

He speeds off before I can scold him for using Corbin's nickname for me.

Back inside, I drop the bags in the kitchen and turn on Corbin with my hands on my hips.

He has the audacity to burst out laughing.

I almost bust a blood vessel in my forehead. I can feel it. It's completely beyond me how the two of them could be so *reckless and stupid.* Don't they know better? Or if they do—why on God's good Earth would they even consider doing something so dangerous? I take a deep breath.

They do ride motorcycles. One of them, without a helmet.

I only get angrier at the thought.

"What were you *thinking?*" I ask Corbin.

"I wasn't," he says through sloppy snickers. He wipes at a tear in his eye. "I only had one."

"You're not supposed to be drinking!"

"Tell me something I *don't* know…" Corbin rests his head against the back of the couch and continues to chuckle. "Hell, Kat, give it a rest. Come here. You can finish the rest of it." He waves his hand at a beer can on the foot table.

I pause, considering it. Then I give in, grab the can, and down the rest of the beer. I collapse onto the couch beside Corbin.

"I didn't even drink a full one, if that makes you feel better. I remembered, after a few sips."

"Sips?" I challenge.

"Swallows." He laughs.

"No more drinking."

"No more drinking," he agrees.

I close my eyes and rest back against the couch. I think of everything I need to do today, of preparations I need to make on the house. All I can think of is the magnitude of the storm approaching, of the way it'll batter the island. I need sandbags. I need to board the windows. Locals have already started to evacuate. All I'm doing is sitting around playing *parent* to Corbin and his friends.

Corbin squeezes my shoulder lightly.

I relax at the feeling. Let all the responsibility fall away for a moment.

"Breathe, Katrina."

I focus on his voice, his command. I breathe.

There will be time for everything, tomorrow.

Chapter Twenty-Six

CORBIN

KATRINA DRANK THREE MORE CANS of beer before we finally called it a night and left the weather channel playing in the living room. She guides me to the bedroom, splays me across the bed gently, then removes each piece of my clothing with precision that should scare me.

Then, she peels each layer of her own clothes away—maxi dress first, sea-shell socks next, then each scrap of lace covering those last bits. She does it all with her eyes locked on my face, reading each and every emotion that crosses my eyes, my lips, my tongue.

I gaze up at Katrina as she straddles me. I place my palms on her thighs and run them up to her hips.

She looks at me with a hazy expression, lips barely parted and shining from each of our frantic kisses. Her hair tumbles down her shoulders in cute spirals, drawing my eyes lower. She teases me with kisses anywhere but my mouth—my cheekbone, my nose, my chin. My neck. My collarbone. Lower.

My eyes flit closed. Warmth spreads through me in time with each breath of hers that spills over my skin. *She knows me so well.* Every movement, every carefully placed kiss. All to undo me.

I want to grab her and roll on top of her and have my way with her. But thanks to the pain still deep-set in my bones and the bulky cast on my leg, most of our nights are spent like this—with her pursuing my pleasure when I should be pursuing hers.

All in good time.

When we finish, I pull her down into the bed beside me.

Katrina pants, her breath cooling my skin and the sweat that's beaded on my chest. Her distant eyes find mine and stay there, searching for something deep in mine.

I brush a stray curl off her sweaty forehead, plant a kiss there.

"I think I love you," she whispers, breathless.

I stare at her, then at her lips, trying to make sure I heard her right.

As if she can read my mind, she says it again, "I think I love you."

"Well," I breathe the word back. "I *know* I love you."

Her face turns even more pink—a blush settling over her sex flush. She almost pulls away. I can feel it in the tension of her muscles, the way that her jaw sets when she puts her mind to something. She's steeling herself. She's readying herself to leave.

"It's okay, Katrina," I say. "Just stay. I'm not going anywhere."

Her muscles unwind, cautiously, like a cat that's unsure of her current situation. Her golden eyes close, and her face clears of emotion. Slowly. It's like watching the sun set on the horizon. I can tell the exact moment when the exhaustion—and the three beers—claim her. Her consciousness slips underneath her wild hair, her petal-pink lips, the sky of freckles on her face. Peace replaces it; it's my favorite thing to watch, even more than the sunrise or the night sky.

I could stay here forever.

Outside, the wind howls ominously, as if trying to remind me of what's coming.

Part of me wants to pack up and leave. Part of me *knows* that storm is nothing good.

But if I can weather the storm in my arms, I know I can weather anything else life has to throw at me.

SUNLIGHT SPILLS ONTO THE BED, soaking the sheets in gold and warmth. It illuminates my surroundings—and the empty spot on the bed next to me. I sigh and rub my face aggressively with my hands. I should've seen it coming. I should've known after something like that, she would run off again.

Irritation tickles some hidden part of my heart.

I shouldn't have to wait, wondering if you want me, Kat.

I don't think that's too much to ask.

I pull myself out of bed, grab a pair of sweats, and wander the house in search of her. I find a note on the kitchen counter that says:

I needed some plywood for the windows. Can you text Nathan and Beatrix and see if they would help me board the windows for the storm?

P.S. Hurricane party at your rental?

It calms my nerves a little, but not completely. What happened to sharing mornings together? I guess, in the end, it means more to me than it does to her.

I text Nathan and Bea in our group chat and wait for them to respond.

RAPTURE RIDERS

BEATRIX

> I MIGHT BE ABLE TO RECRUIT SOME
> HELP FROM THE GUYS AT WORK

NATHAN

> AW, HELL NO. DON'T BRING THEM
> INTO THIS…

BEATRIX
SO WHO'S DOING THE HEAVY LIFTING THEN?

NATHAN
YOU

BEATRIX
NO U

CORBIN
CAN YOU GUYS STOP FIGHTING AND TELL ME WHETHER OR NOT YOU'RE WILLING TO HELP? IF YOU'RE NOT, I'M JUST GONNA HAVE TO HIRE SOMEONE TO COME OVER.

BEATRIX
WE'LL DO IT

NATHAN
FUCK

CORBIN
SEE YOU GUYS TONIGHT

I open Katrina's text string next and tell her Nathan and Beatrix volunteered to help. She reads the message almost instantly, but that's all she does. She leaves me on read. I groan inwardly, then outwardly, then press my palms into my eyes. *This is killing me.*

I spend the next couple hours cleaning up around the house as best I can—collecting our clothes off the floor, washing a load of laundry, running the tiny dishwasher in the alarmingly coastal kitchen. I fold a few towels and tidy up her counters, dump all lingering beer cans, then finally crash on the couch for a break.

My eyelids are growing heavy by the time Katrina comes through the front door, more plastic bags in her hands. Suddenly, all the tiredness leaves my system, as if just the sight of her is a shot of adrenaline straight to my heart. Wind whips her curls up and around her face, and a few stray leaves blow in around her ankles.

I sit up and watch her come in. I offer to help, but she turns me down with a quick, "No," then proceeds to juggle more things in her hands and arms than should be humanly possible. I keep watching her, and I can feel the tension in the room tick *upwards* ever so subtly.

"What?" she snaps. "Why are you staring at me like that?"

I sigh and run a hand over my face. "Like what, Katrina?" I ask. My voice is dull, tired.

"Like you have something to say."

I bite the inside of my cheek. *That's because I do have something to say.*

The red sleeves of her maxi dress are off-shoulder, hugging her arms with frills in the elastic. The dress opens up in the front around her knees, then swoops low in the back around her heels. The color fades, the lower the dress goes, as if someone dumped a bucket of red wine over her head. Normally, I would say the pinkish color at the hem of the skirt wouldn't suit her—that it's too close to the orange of her hair or the blush of her skin—but somehow, she pulls it off. I think it's the red. She's always looked good in red, as if the color was made for her and her alone.

"Say it, Ben." Katrina puts the bags on the floor and puts her hands on her hips. Brown-painted stiletto nails dig into her hip. Her neck is tense, muscles taught. From her neck, all the way down to her hands.

I breathe deep, try to steel myself like she does so well. I know in the end it will be worthless. There's no easy way to have this conversation, and even now, I know exactly how it will go. "Where were you this morning?" I ask.

"I had to get supplies."

"Kat, you never let me wake up next to you the morning after we have sex."

"*So?*" Her voice tilts aggressively, and the conversation tips sideways. This is where it all falls down. "Why does that bother you?"

"Because! I don't know!" I throw one hand up, balancing my crutch hazardously under my armpit. "It matters to me! Is that such a problem—that I want to wake up next to the woman I love?"

"You do."

"Sometimes," I argue, "but never after sex."

"I don't know what to tell you, Ben. If it bothers you that much, then maybe it won't work out between us."

"Kat." I hobble forward. "I *want* it to work out between us. Please try to understand. It's important to me." I reach for her hand and she lets me take it. Her fingertips are icy in my palm.

"Okay," she says. She doesn't meet my eyes. "But," a pause, "please… Please understand that's going to take me time. I don't… I don't ever want to wake up in the bed alone, so it's just easier if I leave first."

"*Katrina,*" I plead. "I'm *not* going anywhere. I will be there when you wake up."

Her eyes fix on me, and something inside me cracks under the pressure of his gaze. "Give me time, Corbin."

"I will. I just want you to *trust* me."

"I'm doing my best," she says through her teeth.

I let her pull her hand out of mine and take the bags to the kitchen table. She unpacks some screws and a measuring tape. The gray plastic bags lay forgotten and deflated on the floor.

"Have you considered…"

She stops at the sound of my voice.

"Evacuating?"

Katrina winces.

"It's just—"

"It's just that you want to leave, right? Something scary comes along, and you go running with your tail between your leg. Right?"

"Katrina, I wouldn't even *be here* if it weren't for you."

"Then leave!" She shouts. She turns on me with tears in her eyes and fire on her cheeks. "Better you do it now than later."

"Katrina—"

But she's already whirling around, storming towards the door. She swings it open to find Nathan and Beatrix there—wide-eyed and alarmed—then stomps right past them.

I move as fast as I can towards the door.

Katrina flees across the small street to the other side where homes are tucked side by side and a walkway lets out into the sand. She knows I won't be able to follow her onto the sand with crutches, but I'll be damned if I don't prove to her *now* that I have no intention of leaving her side—whether that's on the road evacuating or with her in the rental.

"Help me," I beg Nathan.

He looks back at me with a firm expression and a short nod. Beatrix takes my crutches and puts them inside as Nathan loops an arm under mine and helps me across the street. We follow in Katrina's wake, our feet feeling the resounding *thump-thump-thump* of hers as she runs down the boardwalk ahead of us.

"Holy hell…"

"Just don't…" I beg Nathan.

He helps me hobble a little faster.

I don't know what I can do to prove it to Katrina. I've done everything I can think of, and even through my own frustration, I've always put her heart first, as best I can. I think of words to say to her as I struggle after her onto the soft, white sand. Sweat beads on my neck, my chest, under my arms. The tacky, salty air sticks to my skin and hair and makes me want to jump in a shower immediately. But not until I have *her*.

Katrina slows at the water's edge, right where the waves crash. Right where she knows I can't follow.

I get as close as I can, and Nathan stays tucked under my arm, refusing to move even when I tell him to get lost so we can talk privately. He just shakes his head and glares at Katrina.

"Katrina…"

"Go away, Ben!"

"Listen to me, Katrina…"

She swears at the clouds in the sky, the deep bluish-purple storm front moving across the horizon. White peaks crash beyond her, then right before her, soaking the edge of her dress.

"I love—"

"Just stop! Just *listen*, okay?"

I stay silent.

"You say you love me. I get that. But I never knew my real parents, and *every single foster family*—" she says the words slowly, drawing them out with a voice that's breaking and falling like the waves at her feet—"they *all* gave me up. They all said that. They all told me they loved me, that they would love me for a long time, that they would stay with me, by my side… None of them did, Corbin! None of them! They all lied!" Her voice is raw with emotion.

Again, *fuck*, *again*, I'm at a loss for words. Because what could I possibly say to that?

"I have never—*never*—been in a real relationship. Of *any* kind! How can I possibly know that you mean what you say?" She doesn't turn to face me. Her hair coils in the wind—winding then unwinding then winding again. Tangling, like her words, like my emotions.

How could someone stand to hurt her this bad? To ruin her future like this? What did she do to deserve this?

By some miracle, the words form. "You won't. You won't ever know, until you let me prove it to you. Stop pushing me away, and let me show you that real love exists."

"But how can you possibly love me? When no one else did?"

"Seriously, Katrina?" I fight an exhausted laugh. "All this, over that? You think I can't love you because your foster parents were shitty excuses for parents? Who gives two fucks what they think about you!"

"I…"

"Katrina, you're the only reason I'm still *here*. I'm here because I want *you*."

"Corbin," she says, her voice weak, gravelly. "I don't know how to love you, because I never learned to love…"

Something inside me breaks at the sound of her words. Of course. It makes sense. Her flighty nature. Her openness about one-night stands when we first started dating. The way she can never sit still in one life too long.

"Let me teach you," I beg.

Nathan's lips flicker, pressing together to hide an oncoming laugh. I can read his expression: *That's the corniest shit you've ever said.*

I elbow him as hard as I possibly can without shoving myself out of his arm and into the sand. I shoot him a warning glare that says, *I swear if you laugh, I'll skin you alive, dude.*

Nathan just hides his stifled laugh behind an infuriating smirk.

Chapter Twenty-Seven

KATRINA

MY HEART FEELS LIKE IT'S lodged in my lungs.

Corbin stands there, his face crestfallen and his eyes brimming with helplessness. Nathan—the damn bastard—is trying to swallow a shit-eating grin beside him. It's almost enough for me to launch myself at Nathan and get into a full knock-down-drag-out fight.

Hot tears burn my eyes as I glare at them. I'm about to take off stomping down the gray beach when Corbin bolts out of Nathan's arm and reaches toward me. I'm left with nothing to do but grab him and anchor him before he falls. His breath washes over me, making another wave of emotion swell in my chest.

"Katrina, wait. Please. Listen," he begs again. "I love you. Loving you it's—it's like the ocean following the tide. It's part of who I am. I can't *be* the ocean without the tide. I can't be *me* without loving *you*. You don't have to know how to love me now." His words are warm on my face. "That's okay if you can't. Good things come to those who wait."

"Good things come to those who *work* for it, Ben."

"Then work for it," he says. His eyes plead with me, the warm brown color of his irises peeking shyly out in the hazy light of the storm above us.

As if on cue, his reassurances are met with another crash of fear inside me. The temperature drops, all around us, at least ten degrees as the storm inches closer by the second. Chills spread over my arms.

A low rumble of thunder sounds in the distance.

Corbin rubs my arms to warm me.

His presence is nothing if not steady. He's as true as the ocean—as wild and constant and untamed—but always there. It's like looking in a reflection of my own soul, looking at him. It's something I think I could learn to love again, his familiarity, his promise. Because if he's the ocean beneath me, I'm the storm in the sky—and he holds me in light refractions on broken waves. If he exists in the ups and downs of the current of life, then I am the one who paints the color over both of us, leaving us red with fury or deep purple with pain. If I feel it, he feels it too.

Wind lashes my hair against my face.

It will rain any moment.

"Please, Katrina… I would do anything…"

I look over Corbin's tall shoulder to find both Nathan and Beatrix sitting straight on the sand at the edge of the dune, shamelessly watching. Mortified, I refocus my attention on Corbin's off-white tee.

"If you can work for it, I can wait for it."

All I can manage is a nod.

ONCE THE FOUR OF US are back on my side of the road, Beatrix and Nathan help board up my windows and load any remaining storm supplies into the back of my car. They're quiet all along, much thanks to Corbin's death glare any time either of them so much as opens their mouths. They do as they're told, quickly and efficiently. With the rain on and off, Nathan and Beatrix are soaked to the bone, and even Corbin and I have damp hair from our trips in and out of the house.

Finally, when all is done, the four of us stand outside my little rental cottage. Even though it's not truly *mine*, this place has homed so many new, cherished memories, even within the short amount of months I've stayed here. Here, I learned how to be free. Here, I learned how to begin to trust. Here, I learned that I can be open to love. The way the sunlight slants through the windows and the way the white gravel crunches under my feet will always be close to my heart here. I close my eyes and say a silent prayer that the storm will spare this little slice of heaven for me, that when this is all over, I can come back to the small one-bed, one-bath house and make more life-long memories.

With Corbin's wheelchair loaded into the trunk of my car, and him loaded into the passenger seat, I close my car door. I watch as Nathan and Beatrix ride their motorcycles off my driveway and onto the road. The small, dark space of the car cabin is close and humid with our breaths, the windshield fogging lightly. It still has that new car smell, after a year of owning it. I turn the car on, and it dings lowly in response, a subtle rumble below us. I fix the air to defog the windshield. Rain patters on the glass, the road ahead of us.

"Are you sure you don't want to evacuate?" Corbin asks. "We still can."

We.

I don't know how to respond, still, so I just shrug. Sure, I want to leave. Hurricanes terrify me, even though you'd never catch me telling that to Corbin and *especially* not Nathan. But part of me—that reckless, danger-seeking, wild side—wants to see what it's like. I want to see the power go out. I want to see the trees bend in the force of the wind. I want to stand on the beach and let the world show me how scary it can be. Because even then, even in the midst of all that, I would still feel safer, more *seen* than I do in my day-to-day life.

The radio mumbles back some information about the hurricane, as if it wasn't already on my mind. I shut the radio off and sit in silence with Corbin.

"I'm sorry," I say, "for earlier…"

"You don't need to be sorry for the pain that was inflicted on you." Corbin rests his hand, palm up on the center console. For me.

Carefully, I place my hand in his.

He squeezes gently; in my peripheral vision, a small smile. "I'm here for you, if you ever want to tell me…about it. About anything."

I nod. Tears sting my eyes for what feels like the hundredth time today. "I do. Eventually."

"Good things come to those who wait," Corbin says, smile growing.

I can't help but smile a little at his words.

I put my car in gear and get us on the road. The sooner we're hunkered down in his rental, the sooner he and I can settle into a round of drinks and more conversation. Just like the watery road before us, it's hard to see exactly where this will go. But there's one thing I know for sure: Corbin has no intention of leaving my side, no matter what comes our way.

Chapter Twenty-Eight

CORBIN

By the time all four of us have hauled all supplies—and ourselves—into the rental, we're all plastered with rain. I hate the feeling of my pants sticking to my legs, and I *do not* look forward to trying to peel my pants off and over my cast. It won't be long until I'm out of the cast, but every passing moment has me itching to rip it off. It's a good thing that between Katrina and Nathan they've both had a close eye on me, because otherwise, it might've already happened.

Stray rain runs out of my hair and down my neck as I step into the AC one last time. Freezing air rushes over my damp skin, and I instantly hate my situation even more. It must show on my face, because Beatrix is laughing when she looks at me.

"Hell, Ben, just go jump in the shower. You'll be warm in no time."

"Bro, you look like a wet dog," Nathan adds.

"Where's the shower?" Katrina asks.

"Down the hall and to the right," I tell her.

She grabs my hand, throws it over her shoulder, and leads me that way.

Nathan lets out a catcall, and Beatrix punches him in the shoulder. "Ow!"

"Leave them the fuck alone," Beatrix snaps.

We round the corner.

"Y'all are stuck here with us, by the way!" Nathan hollers down the hall. "No escape!"

Katrina flings the shower curtain open and bends over in front of me. I try (and fail) not to look at the curve of her waist and ass as she stops the tub and fills it with water. "I know you can't soak, but I'm going to."

I lean against the bathroom sink and watch her.

The tub is easily wide enough for both of us to sit in together; I want nothing more in this moment to rip the cast from my leg and jump into the bathtub with her, but instead, I watch her prepare her tub in uneasy silence. "This is cruel," I say finally.

"What you and Nathan did to me earlier was cruel." Water splashes behind her. "I needed my space."

"Yeah, right. Last time I gave you your space, you moved five states away. I learned from my mistake, and *you* lost your right to 'space.'"

Katrina shoots me a warning glare.

I just roll my eyes. "You know what I mean."

"No, I don't," she says. She turns and sits on the edge of the tub, arms crossed tightly over her chest. "Please, explain."

I stand and walk slowly to her. The water in the bathtub behind her lets off a small amount of steam, warming the surface of my skin. "You're losing the bet, Katrina. And that means, pretty soon, I get to propose."

"Please do tell me how you think I'm losing the bet." Her dainty chin points up towards me, eyelashes still clumped from her tears and the rain.

"You're just as wild as ever. And you're still right by my side."

"And *you* just said you're not letting me out of your sight."

"I said I'm not giving you your space going forward. It's different."

"It's controlling," she argues. Her bottom lip juts out just enough to make me think she's only entertaining this debate in order for me to kiss her.

"You have a problem with me being in control?" I lean a little closer.

"Only outside of the bedroom," she whispers back with lust glowing in her eyes.

I must lean just a little too far, because all of the sudden, I lose my balance on my good leg, and I teeter into Katrina and knock us both straight into the bathwater. Water goes *everywhere*.

"Oh *god*, Bea, they're at it again!" Nathan moans from the living room.

After Katrina has had her bath and I'm all dried off from our mishap, we sit in my bedroom with Katrina's teal blue overnight bag in the corner and her pajamas laid out on the bed. She closes the door and takes the towel off her body. I can't help but stare—because just like the sunrise or the sunset or the gleam of the moon on the sea, I can never get tired of watching her. I've found, that over our time in the past few months, that cameras can't *capture* her beauty. She is just as wonderful and amazing as all the stars in the sky—and we all know that cameras can never *truly* capture the astonishing beauty of any part of nature. Why should she—as a human— be any different?

Katrina pulls on her camisole and her shorts, the white, eyelet lace on the edge of the light blue pajamas laying flat against her starry-sky skin.

I'm already in my own pajamas—some gray sweats and a black tee—lying on the bed. Nothing has felt better than this moment, save for the constant dull ache in my leg. Rain patters against the rooftop, shuffles the palm tree leaves outside my bedroom window. The wind picks up every now and then and bends the trees ominously in the distance. Pines sway, clouds race. It makes me a little skittish at first, but as Katrina nears the window and peers out, my pulse slows ever so slightly.

"Does it scare you?" I ask her, curious.

Her features betray nothing, but that's how she is more often than not. "Only a little."

"Were there any hurricanes before I got here?"

"No," she says. "Hurricane season starts in June and ends in November. We're in the thick of it now."

I watch Katrina pull her fingers through her wet hair then squeeze it in her towel. Her hair looks darker wet, almost brown, and it makes her complexion look paler, her eyes look darker and bigger. The contrast in her features is striking, something I only saw in Chicago on the infrequent nights she let her guard down enough to shower at my place. Down here, in this unfamiliar rental, it makes Katrina look vulnerable and new. She looks up at me, and my breath catches in my chest.

"Does it scare you?" she asks.

At first, I'm at a loss for words, still stunned by her beauty. "Yes. We don't get wind *quite* like that in Chicago…"

"Are you saying Florida wind puts the Windy City to shame?" A crooked smile crosses her face.

"More or less."

She laughs, and I laugh too.

"Katrina…" I start again.

"No," she says. She hangs her towel on a hook on the back of the door then comes to sit on the bed beside me. In the low light of the day outside—the hazy purple-blue cast it leaves on the room—I feel closer to her than ever, as if we're the only two that exist inside this moment.

Katrina sits on her knees by my own knees, facing me as I rest against the pillows on the headboard. "Let me start. Let me say something first…" Her eyes are downcast. She pulls my hand into her line of vision and traces the veins on the surface of it. Then, she traces lines between the big, dark freckles on my own skin. *You have constellations, too,* her voice haunts me, a memory of our past life.

I wait patiently for her words to come. After all, we have all the time in the world right now. Such an endless feeling in such a fleeting moment. I try with everything in me to hold onto this second, this memory in the making, and etch it into my mind. I want to be able to come back to his room, this time every time I want peace, because *this feels like peace.*

The calm before the storm is always the most I've felt at peace.

"You know I grew up in the system. You know, I'm sure, how hard that can be on people."

I decide to say nothing, just to listen. I squeeze her hand, and she continues.

"That's all they ever say though, that it's hard on kids, on the adults they become. But what they don't tell you is the stories." Katrina rubs her thumb across my skin a little harder. "They don't tell you how some of the families use you for money, and how instead of buying you a new set of shoes, they buy themselves more liquor. How they blame you for their problems. You're always the problem and never the solution. Most of the families don't care as much as they should. Some of them do, I'm sure, but I was never lucky enough to be picked by any of those families… I," her voice cracks, "I envy those who were. I wish I could have had a good family."

A tear falls on my hand.

The rain picks up outside.

A battering of teardrops on the windowpane and a swipe of her palm against her cheek.

"I want to tell you about each of my families," she says with a sniffle. "Maybe not tonight, but in time. I trust you, Corbin, but it's hard to fight twenty-eight years of self-preservation and habit."

"I know," I whisper. "I'm sorry."

"What for?" she asks bluntly, tiredly.

"For everything, Katrina. For what happened to you. That I can't change the past for you. That I made your present somewhat hard to navigate. That I pressured you…into *us*. I know I don't understand where you're coming from, but it's so hard to love you so much when you're pushing me away and I don't know why."

"I know…" She nods a little. "That's why…I'm really going to try. If you know my families, you'll start to understand. I want you to know. And I want to do better. I don't want to keep pushing you away." Her face crinkles with another sob. "I love you so much too, Corbin. But some days, I just don't know *how* to show you I love you."

I reach over and wrap my arms around her shoulders and pull her into me. "Love me without words," I tell her. "Hold me like this, and that's all I need."

She nods into my chest, her tears warming the fabric of my shirt.

Chapter Twenty-Nine

KATRINA

THE EVENING ROLLS IN WITH foreboding clouds in the sky. A dark shadow has fallen over the house, long before the sun sets, yet with all the danger on the horizon, the sunset itself is more spectacular than anything I've ever seen.

The four of us stand in the small backyard of the rental, staring up at the anomaly above us. The clouds are thin and wispy from the wind, slicing across the sky with the occasional cluster of pebble-like shapes. The entire sky is on fire—a vivid reddish-orange and pink that none of our phone cameras are able to replicate. We've long given up on that and now just stare, watching as it changes slightly with every passing minute.

In the corner of my sight, the hammock on the edge of the property—strung between two towering live oaks—swings viciously in the wind. Palm trees rustle near the house, scraping against the roof and siding. And, for once, it seems like most of the bugs and birds are silent. Everything is waiting, anticipating.

Corbin takes my hand, and I let him wrap his fingers in between mine. Yesterday consisted of a long, late-night talk with Corbin. This morning, everyone woke up with worry in their eyes. The wind kept me up last night, and the others echoed the same.

We spent the day today closing all the storm shutters on the rental. Beatrix set candles all around the house, scattering a few lighters liberally throughout. She had two emergency LED lanterns too, which she left on the coffee table in the living room. Beatrix gave Nathan some orders to fill both tubs and any empty containers—water bottles, large glass food bowls—with water. The kitchen is stocked with four packs of bottled water, at least a dozen gallon jugs, and several packs of beer. If I were more of a native, maybe I could've picked on them, but even *I* don't know what to expect. It seems too, from what I hear locals saying, that this hurricane *shouldn't* be taken lightly. Any direct hit is dangerous. Many people already evacuated.

As the last bit of fire drains from the sky, Beatrix and Nathan head back inside, leaving Corbin and me out in the yard.

Corbin presses a kiss to the top of my head. He breathes in deep. "Are you ready?"

"Ready as I'll ever be."

"We can still leave."

I consider it, momentarily. Our chance to leave is fleeting. *Fast.* Newscasters expect the winds to pick up tonight, which means the bridge to the island will close, and we'll have to ride out the storm no matter what we feel.

Corbin turns me in his hands. One crutch props him up from under one arm.

I gaze up at his dark eyes, his spiky hair swinging around his face.

"Have I proved it to you yet?"

I want to hear his words. I want to tease him, make him think it's slipped my mind. "Proved what?"

"That if we were married you could be just as wild as you are single," he says.

I pause, search his eyes.

He searches mine too in the vanishing light.

"We spent months living together. I gave you the freedom you needed, right?"

"Mostly," I say.

"What if we try it with the ring?" he asks. His eyes glitter mischievously.

A lump rises in my throat. "Ben, I…"

"We can stay engaged for as long as you need," he offers, "and if we need to call it off, we can do that too. I want you, one way or another. It's my way of showing you how much I love you."

"How much did you spend on the ring?" I ask, trying to change the topic to be not-so-serious. I glance at his chest, and sure enough, the ring makes a small bump under his shirt.

"More than your car," he says with a stupid grin.

My stomach bottoms out a little. Part of me feels bad; this man has been walking around with something close to forty grand hanging around his neck. It doesn't surprise me. "That's not a flex, Ace."

Corbin just shrugs. "If you say so, Freckles."

Emotion squeezes my throat. "I'll wear it under a few conditions."

"Shoot."

"You don't get on your knee."

"Done."

"You don't tell the others as soon as we walk in."

"Done. But they'll notice."

"I know," I say, biting my lip. "Lastly, you *never* call me your fiancée. It's too serious. I want to be called your girlfriend."

"What about when we do get married? Can I call you my wife then?"

"No. Girlfriend. Wife is way too serious."

"Fine. Done deal, Kat." Corbin loops the ball chain around his neck on his thumb and fishes out the gold-and-diamond ring hanging there. "What do you say?" He holds it up between us, and it sparkles wildly in the space before his eyes. His eyes gleam equally as bright.

I put my hands on my hips. "We can see how it goes."

Corbin shows his teeth in a wide smile. "I'll take it." Corbin takes the chain off his neck with a move so natural that it finally occurs to me why I've never seen him naked with the ring on his chest. He undoes the chain and holds the ring carefully between his fingers. Even still relying on one crutch, his movements are effortless. Practiced.

Warily, I offer him my hand. I *do* want this, but I can't pretend that there isn't fear involved. To say that I trust

Corbin is to say that he's the *only* one on Earth that I do trust. No one else has ever tried to break down my walls like him; no one else has *wanted* to earn my trust like him. So I'll give him this. I'll let him continue to woo me, because in the end, it's what I want too.

The diamond sparkles on top of my finger, making my stomach do a small somersault inside of me. I've never owned anything quite so beautiful. Never mind something this expensive with little to no practical value. Besides making Corbin happy, I guess.

Corbin replaces the diamond in my sight with his closed eyes and bowed head as he places a kiss across my knuckles. My stomach flutters nervously. As if he can feel my nerves, he wraps his hand completely around mine—conveniently hiding the ring—then guides me back into the house. He grabs a beer from the counter, cracks it open, and hands it to me. He leans in again, this time towards my neck, and whispers a quiet, "*Cheers,*" in my ear, then leaves me standing there with the room-temperature beer in my hand.

I swear I can feel my cheeks heat. Flutters travel a little lower. He always did know how to set my nerves on fire in a good way. I take a few drinks of my beer until I can feel the edge of my nerves wear off. It's inevitable that Nathan and Beatrix will see my ring; it's only a matter of time before they do.

FOR THE FIRST FEW HOURS of the evening, we watch the news updates on the TV. The power flickers a couple times, making me jumpy. I notice that Beatrix is fiddling too. Nathan scrolls on his phone anxiously, turning at every creak of the home around us. Corbin's eyes are mostly trained on me, as if he's forgotten about the fact there's a ferocious storm creeping closer with every second.

At nine o'clock a street patrol happens. It makes my blood run cold.

The first thing we hear is a slow-moving siren. We step outside.

An emergency vehicle is driving no more than five miles per hour down the road. A megaphone projects an ominous, crackling voice telling everyone that this is the last chance to evacuate. At nine-thirty, they are closing the bridge due to high winds.

My stomach bottoms out. Again. Harder.

Corbin squeezes my shoulder.

"Maybe we made a bad call," Nathan mutters.

"Don't be a pussy," Beatrix says back.

"Well," Nathan says with a harsh clap of his hands. "Time to get shit-faced. If I'm gonna die, I'm gonna go out drunk as fuck."

"No one's going to die," Beatrix snaps.

"Okay, *God.*"

Beatrix just groans.

Their voices disappear back into the house as I stay staring at the emergency vehicle and the rain-soaked road around it. Palm fronds litter the road, along with displaced Spanish moss and leaves. Muted greens and grayish blues paint the horizon. The dark skies finally get to me, and I turn back into the house. With all the storm shutters closed, it feels like a cave, like a hideout from reality, as if the storm outside might not really be happening.

"You got the radio?" Nathan asks from the kitchen. He shotguns a beer then burps loudly.

From across the room, Beatrix makes a face that looks as if she's trying desperately not to leap at Nathan and start a fight.

Been there, I think to myself.

"The radio's by the TV," Beatrix says. "Spare batteries are with it."

"So what do y'all wanna do for the rest of the night?" Nathan asks. "Rummy?"

"Euchre?" Beatrix asks looking at me.

I look at Corbin.

"Sleep?" Corbin offers.

I drink from my beer. My mind is barely coherent enough to play Rummy. Never mind Euchre. All I'm thinking is about Corbin, the ring, and the beer in my hand. "Sleep," I say.

"Sleep, huh," Nathan says, wiggling his eyebrows. "Okay, whatever you say, love birds."

Corbin grabs a pack of beer, lifts it at Nathan as if to say, *You're right. So what?* He grabs me in place of his crutch and leads me down the hall to his room, his weight shifting on my shoulder as we walk.

I'm grateful for the lack of their eyes and eliminating the chance of them seeing the ring. I don't think I'm mentally prepared for that yet. "You know you can't be drinking that," I tell Corbin.

"Blackjack Rummy, you and me," Beatrix says to Nathan. She swipes a deck of cards off the coffee table and begins shuffling the deck.

Corbin and I round the corner. He leads me to his room. "I'm just stocking up for you," he tells me.

When we walk in, I find that the whole room is lit romantically with all red candles—placed way too nicely to be done by Corbin himself. On the bed, there are red rose petals;

there is a stray, barren stem hiding in a mason jar of roses beside the bed.

I turn and fix a suspicious glare on Corbin.

He just shrugs and smiles and closes the door behind us.

"They knew. They knew, and they helped you."

"What can I say? My friends have my back."

We spend the next few hours talking—tearing up then tearing each other's clothes off. I tell Corbin about some of my families, even ones I haven't thought about in years. We lay side by side, naked and vulnerable, and he shares about his life too. He tells me how he was never enough for his father, never ruthless enough, never cunning enough.

"My father always said I cared too much," Corbin tells me as the analog clock on his dresser changes to 1 A.M.

"That's a lie," I tell him. The beer in my hand is cool and any aches in my body have been long chased away and replaced by easy, swaying movements. Fleetingly, I think about stepping outside into the storm and seeing how long it takes before it topples me over.

"You of all people," Corbin laughs between drinks of a bottle of water, "*you* don't think I care too much? I chased you to Florida."

"You did not chase me." I lean in a press a kiss to his wet lips. He kisses back, sloppy and lazy. "You came to Florida because you were trying to numb the very thing that makes you, *you*. Why?"

Corbin's glassy puppy dog eyes gaze up at me from his place on the pillow. "Because you didn't want me," he slurs.

"I didn't know what I wanted then, but there was never a moment when I didn't want you." I stroke his face, my fingers catching on the stubble on his chin.

"What do you want now?" he asks.

"You," I whisper.

He pulls me into another passionate kiss. His big hands roam over my bare arms, down my hip and leg, then back up underneath the pajama shorts I pulled on after our last round. "Really?" he murmurs against my lips.

I nod.

Corbin takes my beer and sets it on the bedside table and rolls on top of me.

Chapter Thirty

KATRINA

MY BODY FEELS LIKE LEAD as I sleep. I jolt awake a few times, drenched in a cold sweat, only to be unable to move my arms or legs to pull myself from the dread of my nightmares. Sleep pulls me back under.

IN MY DREAM, AN ALARM goes off across the room. I throw my pink and green duvet cover off and stumble over the long legs of my hand-me-down pajamas. In that moment, I think of my older sister and the pretty lace cami sets she wears. I never get anything like that, but I never go without in this house either. I turn the blaring alarm off with a slap to the little black button on the top of the radio.

I have my own bedroom in this life, but it's not decorated the way I want it to be. I tell myself that that's okay. It was always okay here. I go about my morning preparing for elementary school. I wash my face and brush my teeth. While I'm looking at myself in the mirror, I notice that chunks of my curly hair are missing. I pull on the strands, finding blunt, straight chops in random places. My stomach turns queasy inside me, but I decide to say nothing to my parents. The last time I tattled, my siblings took my scrapbook journal—which held the few good memories I'd compiled throughout the years—and left it in the rain. They told me then, that if I tattled again, they would do worse.

I go back to my room, turn on a few little lamps—one on my brushed-green desk and the other on my bedside table. They illuminate my room of mix-matched items: a green bowl chair, a pink shag rug, black slippers in the corner. I walk to my closet and open the door. My heart sinks at the sight inside.

Little circles of fabric litter the floor. Circles of all colors and textures. I look up. Every piece of clothing on my hangers has holes cut out. Everything I own, destroyed. I dig through the ruined garments with tears in my eyes and find whatever has the least amount of damage to wear. The colors clash terribly; I look awful.

I grab my backpack, rub the tears from my face, leaving red, irritated skin around my eyes. I join my brother and sister by the front door to wait for our parents.

"You're not our sister," my foster sister sneers at me.

My foster brother laughs.

They cut my clothes, my hair, to make me look homeless.

When my parents meet us at the front door, they're horrified. My mother kneels beside me and holds me to her chest. She tells me in rushed words that we'll go to the store today to get me new clothes. My father yells at my siblings. He ushers them out, takes them to school without me.

In the end, a few months later after my foster siblings beat me behind the school—my parents returned me to the system, thinking it would be safer for me there than with their own children.

I feel the bruises they left on my belly, the deep, sour spinning of my stomach.

The next pain is in my head.

A hand cracks across my face. My hands hit the floor, pain shooting up my arms.

"She was fine until you came along! She poured all her energy into you, when she should've been taking care of herself! The stress finally caught up to her and look what it did! You killed her. You killed her," the next foster father yells.

I believe every word that comes out of his mouth. I'd loved this mother. She took care of me like her own, even when he gave me side-long glares and underhanded comments about not belonging, like some sort of stray animal.

She used to brush my hair until all the tangles were gone. She would French braid two columns into my curls, making it beautiful and manageable. I loved her. I loved her so much, and I was the reason she was dead.

My ears ring.

Next family. I stand in the hallway, back pressed against the wall. My new foster parents talk at the dinner table together. I listen to what they say.

'I think there's something wrong with her... The teachers say she can't focus. She doesn't make friends. She doesn't even talk. Why doesn't she talk?"

"She just needs time, honey."

"I don't want a child that can't talk to people. What will our family think? They'll think we're raising her wrong! That reflects on us!"

"No... No, of course it doesn't, babe." His voice was always softer than hers. "The agency told us it would be hard for her. Try to put yourself in her shoes..."

My heart thunders against my chest. Tears burn my eyes.

DARKNESS SWIRLS. I OPEN MY eyes to the sound of the storm raging outside, only to find I'm mistaking the wind for my own wheezing breath. I'm pulled under again.

THIS TIME, IT'S NOT *A memory, it's a dream. Corbin stands in front of me. I'm wearing a maxi dress with crude, jagged holes ripped out of it. My hair falls in choppy, uneven cuts in my face. I hold my dress in my hands, confused. He would never do this to me. I look to him.*

There is desperation in his eyes.

"How could you let this happen, Katrina?"

Let what happen? Let what happen? *I try to say.* Nothing comes out.

I look at my hands again. My red dress is drenched in blood; my hands come away slick and wet. What is happening?

"I thought you loved me," he says.

I do love you! *My lips move. No words breach my lips. What is happening to me?*

A pain in my stomach. An emptiness.

I clutch myself, and the thought manifests, vague and distant. A child. We lost a child. It was my fault we lost the child. Because there's something wrong with me. Because I keep running away. I lost my whole future because I couldn't be like anyone else. Thoughts swim in my head, spiraling, pulling me down, down, down… I can't breathe. I gasp for air, but water rushes in instead.

I'm crying. Tears pouring.

My child.

I would have given anything to hold that child again, tell her she was enough, that there was nothing wrong with her, that it would all be okay, all in good time. Just wait… Good things will come… Give it time…

I WAKE, GASPING. NAUSEA RISES. Water in my throat. I throw the covers off, stumble from the bed. Shuffling behind me. Crutches clattering; footsteps thumping.

I grab at the wall, desperate for the bathroom.

I'm on my knees in front of the toilet. Bleach. Porcelain.

My hair pulled back.

Cool air on my neck.

Splashing.

My stomach cramps, *hard.*

I vomit, over and over again.

"It's okay, Katrina," a soft voice.

"I love you," I say. The words tumble freely, from the dream, delayed. "I do love you, I do, I do, I—"

Corbin hushes me. "It's okay. Just breathe." His fingertips comb loose curls out of my face. He smells like fir and leather and smoke, and my throat tightens violently.

I choke on a sob. My body collapses. All the energy drains completely from my limbs, from my muscles. I slide into his arms, onto the floor. The bathroom rug slips and folds and crumples underneath the dead weight of my legs.

Corbin's arms envelop me. He touches me gently, speaks to me gently. "It's okay," he says again.

Finally, finally, I remember the dreams. The realization drags another broken cry out of me. I wasn't crying over a lost baby, I was crying over my own lost innocence. I was mourning my inner child and everything I lost along the way. Something inside me breaks again, deeper, a fault line in the bottom of the ocean. That chasm opens up, bigger, and drags me down into it.

I let it. I let myself feel it all, knowing I've never allowed myself to do that. I've never mourned the things that were taken from me when I was young. Not like this.

So I let the tears fall, let the storm inside me rage harder, wilder, than the one outside of the four walls of this house. I let it all take me—drowning me in emotion I didn't know I had.

Corbin holds me through the storm.

Chapter Thirty-One

CORBIN

WHEN KATRINA FINALLY CALMS DOWN, I help her back to the bed as best I can. Then I go back to the bathroom, wet two washcloths, then return to her. The rhythm of my crutches on the floor feels as familiar as my heartbeat. Steady. Consistent. I wipe her face with one, then fold the second and rest it across her forehead. Her eyes are puffy, her eyelashes clumped together. Her skin is pale from her new lack of emotion, as if all her crying completely emptied her of everything inside.

I've never seen her cry like that.

I lie beside her, wary. I keep my eyes on her, hoping that she can sleep the rest of the night through. I glance at her bedside table to make sure she has a water there, just in case she wakes before I do. I don't want her to have to search out water mid-hangover in the middle of the night.

I breathe deep to try to calm my nerves, but my heart is still racing a hundred miles per hour after Katrina's sudden scene in the bathroom. My hands tingle with pinpricks of emotion. I thought I could understand the very surface of what she went through, but after tonight, I know that I was very, very wrong about that.

I try to clear my mind and sleep to no avail. Even if I could, it's unlikely I would stay asleep for long with the storm outside.

Wind whistles around the siding of the house; the foundation of the house creaks and groans. Rain hammers against the siding and the roof. I toss and turn in bed, trying to get a grip on my jumpy nerves. Every time the wind changes, I roll over. Somehow, by some miracle, Katrina is passed out beside me.

Some hours later, without realizing, I drift in and out of a light sleep. Things keep waking me—either needing to pick rose petals from under my ears or trying hard to remember fading dreams. Most are memories of my past life with Katrina in Chicago. I wonder if her dreams were the same.

MORNING COMES WITH THE SOUND of a tree cracking and splitting and the ground shaking with a distant *boom*. The house creaks and creaks and creaks, and it makes chills climb my arms despite a sticky heat setting in the air. I sit up, look immediately to my left. Katrina is still fast asleep.

The clock across the room is off, no analog numbers on the black screen.

Despite wanting to be here when Katrina wakes—especially after our recent conversation—I want to check on the others.

I stand, dress, grab my crutches, and venture into the hallway. I notice the bathroom door standing open, the toilet lid up. The toilet wasn't flushed from her midnight episode, so I close the lid and flush it. The sound comes back unfamiliar, wrong, hollow. Water drains, but it doesn't fill back up.

Fuck.

I turn to the tub, grab a plastic cup sitting on the side, and fill the toilet tank with a few scoops of water.

So we've officially lost power. Explains the heat.

In the hall, I find the thermostat dark and the screen clear of numbers.

In the living room, Bea is sitting on the couch alone with a glass of water and a few, melting ice cubes. She looks at me, then looks away, tiredness on her usually sharp features. "Please don't gripe at me for opening the freezer. I'm literally dying. I couldn't sleep all night, thanks to the heat and the sounds of projectile puking."

I laugh lightly, drop into the couch beside Bea. "I don't care if you got a few ice cubes, Bea."

"Good, 'cause I wouldn't care if you did."

"I know."

Beatrix sighs. "How is she?"

"Hungover, probably," I say, even though I'm sure it's much, much more than that.

"The eye of the storm is set to pass over us here in a few hours," Beatrix says. "I might try to get some sleep when it quiets down."

"What happened to the party?"

"You checked out of the party last night, boss. Nate and I had a fucking blast."

I laugh again. I lean my head back against the plush white leather couch.

"Hope it was worth it."

I think of all the things Katrina told me—about her different families, about her regrets, about what she wishes she could have done as a child. I told her we could make a bucket list so that I could make sure she experienced all those things anyway. Katrina told me it wouldn't be the same, but I refused to let her turn down the offer. "It was."

Beatrix smiles. "Did she take the ring?"

"On three conditions." I roll my head to look at Beatrix. She gazes back at me. Her smile is snarky and sly. I've known her for such a long time, even as a child, but we only got close after she joined my motorcycle gang, and I couldn't be happier that I got to know her better. She taught me a lot about how to woo women, and so much of her knowledge is to credit for managing to convince Katrina to give me a shot. "Tell me?"

"She didn't want me down on one knee. She didn't want me to announce it to you guys as soon as we walked in—"

Beatrix snorts.

"Yeah, she figured out it was a setup as soon as we got to the bedroom." I rub the back of my neck.

"The third condition?"

"Even if we marry, I have to call her my girlfriend. No 'fiancée' or 'wife.' She said they sound too serious."

Beatrix laughs. "I mean, girlfriend does sound a lot more fun."

I shrug. "Seems like a fair trade-off."

"I'm happy for you, Ben," Beatrix says.

"Thanks."

"What are your plans for when the rental's up?"

"I have some ideas…"

Beatrix raises an eyebrow at me. "So you're staying here, huh?"

A smile threatens my lips. "I mean, I can't exactly up and leave to Chicago unless Katrina is coming back with me."

"If she wants to stay?"

"I'll stay too," I say. "What about you two? Have you and Nathan talked about what you want to do?"

"Well, neither of us really have much back home. I was thinking of renewing the rental, but it's a little too expensive for me, so I've been looking at other living arrangements. Nathan told me he made a friend over at the bookstore who's looking for a roommate, so he's thinking about renting there after our lease here is up." Beatrix takes a sip of her water. "I'm thinking about renting a studio here on the island. There's a nice place off 14th that has some options coming available in October."

"So you two are gonna stick around too?" I grin.

"What can I say? The ocean calls to my soul," Beatrix says with a chuckle.

"That's great, Bea."

Beatrix grins at me. "Who knows, maybe I'll meet someone here, too."

"What ever came of your bet?" I ask, remembering the ambitious *who-gets-laid-first* bet Beatrix and Nathan made back in April.

"Tied," she grumbles.

I laugh. "Surely you don't mean…"

"*Hell* no. I wouldn't sleep with Nathan even if my life depended on it. It was the Mosley siblings. We met them at the bar one night. Their older brother Ethan was with them." Beatrix smiles slyly. "He's taller than me—talk about *rare* down here—*and* he was into me. When Nathan saw that, he decided to sweet-talk Callie. I can't believe it worked."

"Callie, huh?" My eyebrows raise on my forehead. *Didn't see that coming.*

"Tell me about it." Beatrix covers her face.

"Think you'll see Ethan again?"

"No way. Not like that, anyway. It was a fun fling, but he's not my type." Beatrix finishes her water and walks to the kitchen to refill her glass. "It gives me a little bit of hope, though."

Chapter Thirty-Two

KATRINA

I WAKE TO UTTER SILENCE. For a moment, I think I've slept through the storm, that everything is over, that maybe I've slept for months, and everything has gone back to normal, that Corbin has gone back to Chicago and I'm all alone.

There's a knock on my doorframe.

I look up.

Corbin leans there, crutch in one hand and holding a clear glass in the other. Condensation on the outside of the glass drips onto his fingertips. Only then do I realize how hot I actually am. The sheets are soaked, and my pajamas stick to my skin, uncomfortably damp. "The power's out," Corbin tells me. He limps over and sits beside me, handing me the glass. "Bea got into the freezer to get herself some ice, so I justified getting you a cold glass too. How are you feeling?"

"I'm okay…" I manage with a sore throat. Acid stings the back of my tongue. Slowly, the memories return. The dreams. Vomiting in the middle of the night. Passing out in Corbin's arms. "I mean…"

Corbin waits for me to speak.

"I'm not," I say, swallowing a gulp of ice-cold water. It cools my body almost instantly. I drink more. "I'm not," I start again, "but I will be."

Corbin nods.

"It's… It's just a lot. I think, last night, talking to you about all my families… It brought a lot of unresolved stuff to the surface." I pause, watching the ice cubes swirl in my glass. "It's not great, but I think it needed to happen. I just need some time to work through it."

"If you want some space—"

"*No,*" I say too suddenly, too harshly. I take a breath then start again. "No. Please, no. I want you here. It's just…going to take me some time. But I want to work through it with you." I look up at his eyes.

There's a ghost of a smile on his mouth. "Whatever you need, Katrina." He touches the side of my face. "Just warn me when you need a road trip, and we'll go, okay?"

"Deal." I smile weakly. "Thank you, Corbin."

"Want some breakfast?" he asks.

I nod.

"The eye of the storm's over us now," he tells me. "Roads outside are flooded, and there are several big trees down. We're lucky. Some of the houses on this road took some pretty bad damage. We're not quite in the clear yet, though." Corbin watches me stand and squeezes an arm around my side in a small hug before we go to the kitchen. "Beatrix and Nate want to have a *proper* party tonight, if you're down."

"For the tail end of the storm," I guess aloud.

"Yup," Nathan calls from the table. "Euchre this time, bitches." He already has a beer open beside a bowl of boiled peanuts.

I scrunch my nose at the thought of having beer and boiled peanuts for breakfast.

Corbin presses a kiss to my nose. "What do you want for breakfast? We've got junk, junk, and more junk."

"Who picked out the food?" I ask, exhausted.

"You did, girlfriend," Corbin says as he digs through the pantry to pull out a box of vegan cookies. He beams back at me with a smile so bright.

You could get used to that smile.

WE SPEND THE EVENING AROUND the dinner table, a deck of plastic playing cards sticky from boiled-peanut fingers and the alcohol spilled on the table. I try to savor the feeling of it. The house is lit by the white-LED light of storm lanterns and the flicker of gingerbread-scented candles. Beatrix grins and slaps her hand on a card, yelling "Rummy!" loudly and stealing the card Nathan just laid down. Neither Nathan nor Beatrix say anything about the huge, grossly noticeable rock on my finger, but they both steal glances at it every now and then when they think I'm not looking. Despite their undercover stares, they make me feel at home, like I've always been a part of their little biker squad.

For once, I finally feel at home.

Chapter Thirty-Three

KATRINA

TWO MONTHS LATER

I WAKE TO THE SOUND of Beatrix and Nathan screaming at each other, the sound of suitcase wheels rolling aggressively, and the low rumble of curses coming from Corbin. I sigh, hide my head under the pillow, and breathe in the smell of Corbin's cologne on the sheets—that warm, familiar smell of fir and leather and smoke.

This has become my new normal.

Two months ago, after the hurricane, my landlord told me I had thirty days to get out. The cottage I rented had taken too much damage during the hurricane, and the owner decided instead of sinking the money into the home, it would just be listed for sale instead. Thankfully, Corbin offered me a place at his rental and helped me move out overnight. I hadn't moved into the rental with much to begin with; everything fit inside my car, just as it did on the move down.

I returned to my job at the diner on the marina after the hurricane repairs there were done, though the city still argued the building itself was condemned and business should cease immediately. (That's an ongoing issue.) Corbin even took up some side gig helping repair damage done by the storm. Mostly, he volunteered where he was able to, but every now and then he got some cash for his help. All that cash went straight to his friends, whether to take us all out for drinks or to help Nathan and Beatrix pay their new rental deposits.

Life has regained some sense of normalcy.

I've fallen into an easy day-to-day life with Corbin. I even slipped up and called him my fiancé at work—breaking my own rule of never calling him anything more serious than my boyfriend—and Jackson about had a heart attack right then and there at the bar counter.

The front door slams in the distance.

"Morning, Freckles," Corbin says from the doorway. He leans against the frame, black-clad and arms crossed over his chest. He's finally free of his crutches and now only wears a simple black brace under the leg of his pants.

"Morning, Ace," I grumble from under the sheets.

"C'mon. Get up and get ready for the day. I've got a surprise for you," he says.

I shove the pillow off my head to look at him, but he's already gone. Curiosity peaked, I drag myself out of bed and take a quick shower and get dressed in some jeans and an oversized, vintage tee. I find Corbin in the kitchen, a plate of vegan tofu egg scramble already ready on a plate for me.

"How do you feel this morning?"

I look at him suspiciously as he hands me the plate. "Fine."

"Nate and Bea are moving into their new places today."

"Same day?" I raise an eyebrow.

"Those two can never coordinate well," Corbin says, shrugging.

"That must be inconvenient."

"Do you work today?"

He knows I don't, so I narrow my eyes at him. "What do you have planned, Ben?"

"You'll see," he says with a grin. He sips on a cup of steaming coffee. All around the rental, there are bags and suitcases packed. Corbin and his friends didn't show up with much else but the clothes on their backs, but after six months, they all managed to stockpile small amounts of clothes and souvenirs. I guess they all assumed I would help drive the suitcases to their new places later today, as none of them are able to move much but a backpack on their motorcycles.

Once we finish breakfast, Corbin has me put on a blindfold then leads me outside. He guides me onto the back of the bike.

This time, he skips the helmet.

You must not be going far.

I'm surprised that he would go without for either of us after his wreck, but even I'll admit that I far prefer the feeling of the wind in my hair. He replaced his bike about a month ago, when he was cleared by his doctor to ditch the crutches and graduate to a brace. On the days we ride together, I notice a newfound wariness in his movements, as if he's ready for the worst to happen again.

"Hold tight, Kat," he says.

I grip his chest.

I try to keep track of his turns as we ride across the island. I'm lost after it feels like he does a detour just to confuse me. He never goes too fast, so I know he's using all back roads. The day is cool enough that the heat isn't all-consuming. In the breeze of his motorcycle, it's perfect. Every now and then I feel a slightly colder breeze, a telltale sign that there must be rain clouds somewhere in the sky. Yet, the sun still warms my skin.

Corbin pulls into a gravel lot, stone crunching under the tires of his bike. He parks his motorcycle then lets me get off the end first, holding my hand all the while so I can keep my balance. He positions me on the gravel, hands on my shoulders. Then, his footsteps crunch away. "Okay," he says. "You can take off the blindfold."

I hook my fingers around the top of the blindfold and pull it down around my neck. In front of me, Corbin stands, hands wide on either side of his body. His smile is just as wide.

Behind him on his right is my old rental cottage. On his left, a realtor sign that reads *SOLD* in red and white.

My heart skips a beat. "You…"

"It's all yours, Katrina," he says.

"The jobs…" It comes together. Cover up. All his "jobs" were cover up for what he was really up to. Fixing *this* house. "You bought the house…and fixed it up?"

Corbin nods, smiling even bigger—something that seemed impossible two seconds ago.

I exhale shortly. Rain pricks my skin like chills.

"Say something, Kat," he begs.

"I don't know what to say…" The thought of returning to the little safe space I had found after all the turbulence in Chicago, it felt like coming home. I thought closing the door on the rental when I left a month ago meant I'd be in the wind again for the foreseeable future—especially with Corbin's own rental lease running out fast. This explains a lot, especially why Corbin wasn't at all worried about his expiring lease. "Thank you," I breathe. "Thank you, Ben. This is… I mean, it's entirely too much." *Like the car and the ring,* I think. But this… Somehow this is different.

"I figured you could use a place to call your home."

I run to him and wrap my arm around his neck. *He is your home, but how could you ever tell him as much? Maybe he feels exactly the same as you do…*

"Thank you," I murmur into the soft skin of his neck. I look up at the sky from inside the circle of his arms, blinking away tears. Above us, the sky is storm clouds and baby blue.

Full sun, full rain. In the dark of the clouds above us, the light refracts on the raindrops, making them look like crystalline snowflakes falling from the sky. A distant memory of where we came from. A reminder of home.

Acknowledgments

I WOULD BE REMISS NOT to thank Amelia Island and its people for all of the drama and inspiration that went into the making of this novel.

Thank you to my friends and family for encouraging me to *go for it* with this fun little project. Shout out to my beta readers, too; you guys are the best! And a special thanks to Lori for the pick-me-up texts when *Inheriting Armageddon* rejections get to be too much. Thanks to all of you, I believe in myself as a writer. Now I can say, without a doubt, that I have the grit and resilience (and skill) that it takes.

Thank *you*, dear reader. I'm glad you found this book. I hope that you've grown to love these characters as much as I love them. If you do, I'm happy to tell you, you have at least six more books to look forward to to revisit these chaotic souls.

Lastly, and most importantly, thank you God for the pain and trauma. Because without that, there would have never been this. It's an honor to have honed my artistic inclination of a gift into something (finally) tangible. My art means everything to me, and I would have never chased it like this if it hadn't been a God-given lifeline through the worst of times.

About the Author & Artist

R. D. G. LOVER IS AN ARTIST, author, and freelancer. She owns a small business where she sells her original art and takes freelance work for editing services, website design, graphic design, custom paintings, and more. Lover spends her free time stargazing, singing loudly in her car, and working on her illustrated novels about the Four Horsemen of the Apocalypse. She has made it her goal to write and illustrate a novel in every genre.

Her website, www.4pocalypseArts.com, showcases a gallery of all-original art and writing from her stories. To stay up to date with R. D. G. Lover's future releases, be sure to subscribe to her newsletter on her website and follow her on any social media @4pocalypseArts.